CW00976745

Secrets Among The Shamrocks

By Karen L. Robbins

This novel is a work of fiction. Where real people, events, establishments, organizations, or locales appear, they are used fictitiously. All other elements of the novel are drawn from the author's imagination and all characters are fictitious.

Three may keep a secret, if two of them are dead.

Benjamin Franklin

1

Green.

Never in my life had I seen a place so green. I thought my Florida home was green but this was far beyond the tropical greens of the South. This was green everywhere, trees, grasses, bushes. The only thing not green were the homes but even some of those were partially covered in green ivy.

So, this was Ireland, the Emerald Isle. I sighed.

My eyelids were heavy but I doubted I would fall asleep. Not only was the countryside interesting but my driver, Finn, was driving on the wrong side of the road. At least it seemed like the wrong side but it was only different from back home. Here the left side of the road, not the right side, was the correct side. Would I ever get used to it? What had my daughter, Evelyn, gotten me into?

Evelyn had become Mrs. Charles Walden shortly after her contract with the cruise line ended where she had served as cruise director on the ship named Enchanted. Charles had been the chief of security for the ship and that's how they met. Both decided after several years of being at sea, they would enjoy planting their feet on terra firma.

"All fine Ms Stengel?" Finn asked glancing up in his rear view mirror. He had insisted I ride in the back seat saying it would be easier on my nerves until I got used to being on the left side of the road. Maybe he was right. I found myself staring out the side windows so I wouldn't notice so much which side of the road we were on. I did gasp a bit when I saw how fast he was going but when he saw me looking at the speedometer he chuckled. "Remember, Ms. Stengel, over here everything is in kilometers." I relaxed a bit. He wasn't going nearly as fast as I thought he was.

"I'm fine, Finn," I said, "Thanks for asking. I'm enjoying this beautiful countryside."

"Aye, that it is," Finn said nodding his head. "And tis a fine day to welcome you with."

Finn seemed as curious about me as I was about him and the country I would call home for a while. He met me at the airport holding a sign that simply read "Ms. Stengel." I liked him from the first moment we met. He wore an ivory colored cable knit sweater with jeans and a flat tweed patchwork cap that partially covered a head of red hair graying at the temples. His red beard was trimmed and accented a wonderful smile. He was a little taller than me, probably around 5'6" but with his ruddy complexion and build, it was obvious he worked outdoors.

When I got into the car, he apologized for not using my whole name on the sign. "Your daughter told me your name was Kathleen Catherine O'Shaughnassy Stengel but I couldn't fit it all on my sign." I explained that everyone called me Casey and he could as well but he still insisted on Ms. Stengel. He had no idea who Casey Stengel the baseball player was so I had to explain and then tell him I wasn't related anyway. My last name came from my husband, Paul, who had passed away several years ago.

Maybe he would call me Casey after we got to know each other better. Finn worked for Evelyn and Charles in the gardens of the castle and lodge where they were establishing a bed and breakfast. My job would be to organize the household things and lend a hand getting the rooms ship shape. With my experience as a household manager, Evelyn thought I would be an excellent asset, or so she said to flatter me into accepting the position at least for a while. I never had any experience with a bed and breakfast operation. None of us had. So we found a short seminar in what we needed to know before coming over to Ireland. It covered basics. Bookkeeping, guest registration, menus, ordering household supplies. I was pretty sure supply ordering would be easy enough for me. I'd managed enough households to have a good idea of the needs. This would be different though. More people and they wouldn't live there, just come and stay a time and leave. I took a deep breath. I can do this I told myself. Evelyn needs me and I can do this.

On our way from the Shannon Airport, we'd passed through a city called Limmerick and then through a town called Tralee. I loved the names of the Irish towns. They seemed whimsical and melodic not like baseball player nicknames but every bit as creative. The bed and breakfast castle that Evelyn and Charles were to manage was near a town called Dingle. It sounded fanciful.

Our route took us past a shoreline before turning inland again and soon I saw signs that indicated we were near Dingle. The car slowed and Finn pulled to the side of the road. I leaned forward and looked out the front window. From this spot on the hillside we could see below us a harbor area. It looked so peaceful. The green of the land met the blue of the sea. Sea birds glided below the puffy white clouds that dotted the sky. I sighed.

"It's amazing," I said. "Beautiful. Serene. Peaceful."

"Aye," Finn said, "Tis been my home since I was a wee lad." He nodded his head in appreciation as his eyes swept the view. "Well, we'll drive through and then I'll have you at the Castle Shamrock a few minutes after that." He started the car again.

I sat back in the seat. I was going to enjoy this. I could already see that it had none of the hustle and bustle of the Florida home I'd left. All my things were put in storage back there. I didn't know how long this new life would last and my things would be there for me if and when I needed to return. My friend, Max Dugan, helped me pack everything up. He would be coming here soon as well. He had finally quit the county sheriff's homicide department. When Charles learned that Max was quite a handy man, he asked him to join us in this new venture. Max agreed. I was glad. Things seemed to be working out well for the two of us as we got to know each other better. I hoped the relationship would flourish as well as all these healthy green plants I saw around me.

My hand on the back of the front seat, I leaned forward a bit. "Finn, are there a lot of shamrocks at the castle? Is that where it got its name?"

Finn chuckled. "No. Actually Shamrock is its new name. Before this it was called Castle Glas. Glas is the Irish word for green so it hasn't changed too much since shamrocks are green clover. When the new owners bought the old castle I guess they thought the name Shamrock would bring in more tourists. It's all about marketing nowadays. There's not a lot of clover to be had on our rocky land."

I sat back. No shamrocks at Castle Shamrock? Maybe we could do something about that. I caught one more glimpse of the harbor as Finn turned the car away from the water's edge. We climbed a bit again and suddenly there it was, a castle! But what a sight. Half of it was in ruins. My heart sank. This was our bed and breakfast?

2

The lane we turned onto as we neared the castle was closely lined on both sides with hedgerows. I learned from Finn that was the term for the rows of bushes and small trees that crisscrossed the fields of green. Originally they had been planted back in the 1800s to mark land ownership and to keep cattle from roaming. It was difficult to see anything through the tall thick growth. Then, just as I felt a bout of claustrophobia coming on, we turned again through a break in the hedgerow and the castle was before us.

As castles go, it wasn't that large. It was constructed of huge stone blocks many of which had fallen and rolled away from the part of the castle that still stood. Again I wondered how we were to make a bed and breakfast out of it. But then Finn drove around the back of the castle and a lovely quaint building came into view. This must be the lodge Evelyn and Charles spoke of. Yes, now this could be a bed and breakfast. It was beautiful.

The lodge was made of grey stone. Ivy covered several outside walls. It was huge by my standards. While I was household manager for a couple of what I would call mansions or estates, none of them compared in size to this. Was I really ready for this new job?

I got out of the car and stood for a moment taking it all in. There were two floors but the building sprawled in every direction. According to Evelyn there were twenty bedrooms. Several of those would be for us but the rest would accommodate our guests. The windows were tall and I guessed that the ceilings inside would be as well. As

I did a turn around, I noticed some beautiful flowers blooming along the hedges that lined the drive at the front of the lodge.

"Finn, is that your handiwork?" I asked as I pointed to the colorful blooms.

"'Tis my planting but God's handiwork," he said with a grin. "Springtime brings out the best colors."

I was about to ask him more about the flowers in the yard but I was distracted by a small black and white dog running toward us barking for all it was worth. It stopped short a little ways from us and crouched down, tail wagging faster than a batter taking his warm up swings. The face was black with a white stripe that ran from the top of the head to the nose. The neck was a ring of soft white fur against a black back that continued down the chest to white legs and feet. A patch of white fur tipped the end of the wagging tail that seemed to indicate a desire to play.

Finn put one knee down and patted the grass beside him. "Come here Allie. Meet our new friend." The dog bounced happily to Finn then began to circle me, sniffing to see that I was indeed friendly. I held my fist out to let her sniff before I tried to touch the soft fur.

"She's beautiful. A border collie?" I asked as I ran my fingers through the soft mane on the back of her neck.

"Aye," said Finn. "She came from O'Malley's farm. His Katie had more pups than he could handle and he gave it to Miss Evelyn as a welcome gift. She's a handful sometimes. Still a pup at heart and has some growin' and learnin' to do."

Allie's ears perked up and she turned abruptly to run over to the corner of the lodge. Finn and I turned toward the noise as well just as Charles appeared, struggling with a huge ladder. He was dressed in an old pair of jeans and sported a tee shirt that read "Walk the deck for the cure." It was from a fund raising event during his days as security chief on the Enchanted. Now my son-in-law is no slouch. At six foot and with broad shoulders it was a surprise that the ladder was getting the better of him. In all fairness, it was a big ladder. Finn immediately ran to help him. "Mr. Charles, I told you to wait. I would help with that."

Charles chuckled. "Finn, I thought I could handle it but you were right. This ladder has a mind of its own." He looked over at the car. "Casey! You're here!" Charles asked Finn to help hm set the ladder down. He brushed back the wayward dark curls that had fallen over his forehead and walked over to me to give me one of the warm hugs I had grown to love from my new son-in-law. "How was your flight?"

"Long but the drive here was wonderful." I nodded at Finn. "My driver was excellent and most informative. I feel I've learned a lot about Ireland already," I said, "and I've received a warm welcome from this beautiful girl." I reached down and scratched Allie behind the ears as she nudged my hand for attention.

Charles laughed. "She seems to have attached herself to you already." He looked up and pointed to a spot just above the entrance. "I've been installing our security cameras."

"Security cameras? Why do we need those? Is this a dangerous neighborhood?" I looked around again. Fields stretched out in several directions with lovely blooming hedgerows marking them. It was pastoral. Didn't look dangerous to me.

He laughed. "No, not a dangerous neighborhood. Our owner company wants them installed. I guess the company's insurance agency is asking for them. Nowadays anyone can claim anything and at least the cameras will help us determine any liability issues should they arise. Besides, they knew you were coming to work here and since you seem to find dead bodies, they decided it would be helpful in solving any murders."

I gave him one of those looks I used to give Evelyn when she was being ridiculous. "That's not funny, Charles."

"Sorry," he said hanging his head like a penitent child but grinning broadly. "Just kidding."

I patted his arm. "But if I find any bodies, you'll be the first to know." He grinned at me.

"Let's get inside," Charles said, "Evelyn's been eager to see you." He looked at Finn who seemed puzzled by the dead body talk. "Finn, we'll leave the ladder for now. Can you bring in the luggage for Casey?"

"Sure," Finn said lifting his cap to scratch his head. "Glad to."

I followed Charles into the lodge. A huge two story foyer greeted us. I couldn't help it. I gawked. Charles put an arm around my shoulder. "It's amazing, isn't it?" He turned me a bit and pointed to the room on our right. "Have a look here at the sitting room. . .or parlor. We haven't decided what to call it yet."

I took a few steps forward and found myself in a huge room that held several cream colored brocade sofas and chairs. The walls displayed some paintings and mirrors that were contained in ornate golden colored frames. At the windows were tall shutters that matched the size of the windows. They were drawn back to let the light in. The whole room was paneled in what looked like oak and accented with moldings and wainscoting. A small alcove held a baby grand piano. Here and there lamps and accessories were arranged to enhance the seating areas. The only word I could think of to describe the whole thing was "regal".

A voice behind me said quietly, "So do you think you can keep this place spruced up?" I turned into the welcome hug of my daughter.

"Oh Evelyn, it's beautiful." I held her away from me for a moment before hugging her again. She was dressed in jeans and a powder blue polo shirt that had the Enchanted logo embroidered on it. She and Charles had left their old jobs with quite a wardrobe apart from their uniforms. Her big brown eyes were sparkling. Her smile lit her face. "And you look even more beautiful."

Charles put an arm around Evelyn. "Her new life agrees with her, don't you think?" They grinned at each other and Charles kissed the top of her head. Evelyn, like me was only about 5'5" and I noticed that the hair that had once been sun bleached by her cruise ship job was returning to a little darker shade of brown, a natural shade unlike her mother's whose color was a store bought Mocha Brown. She had it pulled back in a ponytail, a lot more casual look than the tight knot she had always fashioned at her neck when she was in uniform on the ship.

"I think this new life agrees with both of you." I beamed with love for the two of them. They were great kids. Kids, even if they were in their early thirties. There was a little part of me that wanted to ask if they had any baby plans. After all, none of us were getting any younger and I didn't want to be an old grandmother. But I knew with this new venture, it was not the time to ask.

"Well the new life is agreeing with us so far but then we haven't added any guests into the mix yet," said Evelyn. She gave a little nervous smile. "I get butterflies every time I think about it."

"Honey, you spent all those years entertaining thousands of guests," Charles said. "You'll do just fine."

"I was only the cruise director. I just supplied the entertainment for them. I didn't have to supply their every need. There was a whole crew of others to do that." Evelyn shook her head as she said it.

"Well, isn't that why you hired a Household Manager?" I said laughing. "That'll be a big part of my job. We'll work it out. Just you wait and see."

"Excuse me," Finn said from the doorway as Allie bounded past him and began to pounce on Evelyn. "Ms Stengel, where would you like these?"

"Thanks, Finn. I'll take them from here," Charles said as he turned and smiled at the man who had removed his cap when he entered the house. Such manners, I thought. Max never removed his cap when he came inside.

Of course it didn't bother me all that much since it was a Dodger's ball cap and my loyalty to the team matched his.

My goodness, I had been so busy I hadn't thought about baseball in a couple of weeks. Spring training should be over and the season starting. I needed to get the internet connection set up that Evelyn promised so I could keep up with my team.

I followed Charles down a hallway that led to the kitchen. He set my luggage down and gently guided me into a beautifully designed kitchen more modern than I would have imagined it. A huge island counter was in the middle with a nice array of lights shining down on it. They resembled glass cones and drenched the workspace with light. A small commercial stove with two ovens sat against a wall and a nice sized refrigerator had an ice and water dispenser. Allie disappeared into a little alcove by a door that led outside. I could hear her lapping up water.

A window above the sink gave a view of the lovely gardens behind the lodge that I looked forward to exploring when I had time. How did Finn keep all of that up? I looked down and ran my hand along the top of the dishwasher. Thank goodness we had that as well. A kitchen without a dishwasher would be like a ballpark without a grounds crew.

"It's wonderful," I said to Charles who stood grinning as though he were responsible for the whole thing. In part, he was. He'd insisted the owners update the kitchen and they had agreed that it needed to be more efficient. I'd not seen the kitchen before the makeover but what was here now would work wonderfully.

"Let's get you settled," said Charles as Evelyn came in.

"Mom, I'm going to get us some lunch," Evelyn said. She hugged me again. "Let Charles take you to your room and then join us here." She pointed to a little nook that held a table and six chairs. It looked cozy. "I tried out the Guinness Irish stew recipe we found. I think you'll like it."

"Okay, honey," I said and motioned to Charles. "Lead the way."

Charles took me a little further down the hall and opened a door on the right. He paused and pointed to the door across the hall from mine and said, "That's our suite and you're welcome to come in anytime to join us."

I stepped through the door Charles held open into a beautifully furnished room. A small sofa and a chair sat across from my very own television and off to one side of the room an archway made an alcove where my bed was. I could see a dresser and a closet door to one side of it. And I had a window that looked out on the gardens! "It's perfect," I said trying to keep a tear from rolling down my cheek. At most of my other live-in jobs I'd only had a bedroom and a bath. A bath. Where was the bath? As if Charles knew what I was thinking, he pointed to another small door.

"That's the bathroom. Sorry it isn't bigger but it has a shower, sink and toilet and it's private. When they converted many of the rooms for the bed and breakfast, they had to use a closet to make a bathroom. We had to get armoires to use for closets in some of the rooms."

"It'll do just fine," I said nodding my approval. "Let me freshen up a bit and I'll be out to sample some of that stew."

"I think you'll like it. I didn't know Ev had such good cooking skills." He put an arm around my shoulder and squeezed a bit. "She says she got them from her mother."

I laughed and shooed him out of the room. I wasn't all that hungry since my biological clock was messed up with jet lag but the smell of stew drifted down the hall promising a delicious treat.

Charles and Finn were discussing something at the kitchen table when I entered. I walked to the stove and took in the aroma of a rich Irish stew that simmered on the stove. Charles was right. If this was a sample of Evelyn's skills in the kitchen we would all eat very well.

"Mom, can you help me carry a few plates over to the boys and then we can all sit down and eat?"

"Sure, honey." I carried a large shallow bowl of stew over to each of the guys and then Evelyn and I got ours and sat down with them. Charles bowed his head and said a blessing over the food. I heard Finn whisper a quiet "amen" before we all dug into the lamb and vegetables covered in a thick rich gravy.

"Evelyn, this is perfect," I said savoring my second bite.

"Okay, but what does our real Irishman have to say? Does it pass muster?" Evelyn stared hopefully across the table at Finn.

"Please don't be botherin' me with questions when I'm enjoyin' some of the best Irish stew I've ever had." Finn put another spoonful into his mouth as the rest of us all chuckled.

As Charles and Finn slowed down the consumption of their meal, they began to talk about some of the things that still needed to be done around the castle. "I found another fresh hole," Finn said. "I dunna think it's a stray dog digging. The hole is too clean. More like a shovel made it."

"What in the world would anyone be digging for around there?" Charles set down his spoon and steepled his hands over his bowl. "Don't they realize it could be dangerous if they dislodge some of those stones that have been holding the place together?"

"Perhaps someone is looking for artifacts?" Evelyn offered.

"I can't imagine there would be any artifacts left. The place was pretty much cleaned out when it first started to collapse," Charles said. "That was years ago. The archaeologists gave up on any further searches especially when part of that other wall fell. It was too dangerous and they weren't finding much."

My thoughts turned to the security cameras that

Charles was setting up. "Charles, would anything show up on your cameras? Do you have one at the castle?"

"No. None of the cameras I have for the lodge will fit the bill for the castle and I'm just getting them set up. I was doing a little research and found a trail camera that might do the trick at the castle."

"A tail camera?" I was confused by the term. I had visions of Allie sporting a camera on her tail to keep an eye on the castle.

Charles chuckled. "Not tail. Trail. It's a camera often used by naturalists who want to observe animals. Hopefully we can feed the video to a cell phone or website. I think I have enough in the budget to afford the subscription fee. If not, we'll have to remove the storage disk to see what the camera picks up."

I sat back feeling foolish. Of course. Tying a camera to a dog's tail would be ridiculous. "I'm sorry," I said with a laugh. "Tail camera. Senior moment." I wasn't elderly yet but at fifty-something I was rapidly getting there. "Guess my hearing is going. When are you setting up a camera at the castle?"

"I have it ordered. Just waiting on delivery," Charles said swallowing his last bite of stew. "With any luck, we can discover what or who is digging the holes. If it turns out to be a stray dog, we're hiring him to help us with the landscaping."

Finn looked bewildered and then realized Charles was joking. He gave a laugh and stood up with his empty bowl in hand. "Guess that's my cue to go back to work." He nodded at Evelyn. "Your stew is perfect. Thank you." With that he took his bowl to the sink and rinsed it before he placed it on the counter. Such manners and so helpful. Was Max going to be like that when he got here? I was curious to see how we would get on together on a daily basis. I expected it to be a good test for our relationship.

Manners or not though, Max was a good investigator. Maybe he could help Charles and Finn solve the mysterious digs at the castle.

3

The first afternoon on my new job was spent looking into all the guest rooms in the lodge. I noted which rooms needed my immediate attention if we were going to meet our deadline for our first guest who was due to arrive soon. Several times when I glanced out the window I noticed Finn at work in the gardens pruning and weeding. He was a hard worker. I doubted he needed a sidekick dog to help out no matter how good the dog was at digging.

One of the guest bedrooms in a corner of the lodge on the second floor had a view of the castle. From this side it almost looked whole. I wondered if anything other than old age, had contributed to its collapse. Was there a battle fought here? I made a mental note to check and see if Evelyn had any books on the history of the castle. It would be something I was sure the guests would be interested in as well.

The laundry room was tucked into a corner in the back of the lodge that appeared to be an add on to the original building. There probably hadn't been any place in the original building to house the commercial sized washer and dryer needed should we fill all our guest rooms. Sheets, towels and bedspreads would need to be fresh for each guest's visit and refreshed in the middle of longer stays. Evelyn had already stocked the cupboards with the necessary laundry supplies, laundry soap, softener, and stain remover should we need it. That girl had been busy for sure. Next to the larger machines was a smaller set for our personal laundry. They were a bright pink. I wondered who bought them. Maybe they felt we needed to add a little color to the room. A large cupboard that had a toned down pink color was built into the wall opposite the machines and would hold the clean linens and towels.

I began to unpack some of the sheets from their shipping boxes and load the washer. I didn't want the factory smell of new sheets for our guests but rather the nice lavender scent of the detergent that Evelyn had bought. The washer was easy enough to figure out. I looked the dryer over as well so that I'd know what to set it at when the sheets were washed. As I turned to leave, the phone in my pocket vibrated. I jumped. It was always an unexpected surprise to get a call or text.

The text message was from Max.

Boarding the plane. On my way to the Emerald Isle. Can't wait to see you.

I texted back.

Have a safe trip!

I smiled at the phone. This was going to be quite an adventure living in close proximity to Max. Would our relationship survive? I had met Max when I was a suspect in the murder of my former boss, Mr. Popelmayer, found deceased in his orchid greenhouse and yes, found by me. Max and I had worked together to solve the murder and became great friends. Did I mention we were both Dodgers fans? In the unfortunate incident on Evelyn's cruise ship where I found another body, Max surprised me with a visit and also a proposal. We had a bit of a disagreement when he wanted to rush into marriage but we decided to slow things down and I gave his ring back. Now we were just good friends. Really good friends.

I pocketed the phone and went to the kitchen to see if I could help Evelyn with dinner. I wasn't very hungry but the smell of roasting potatoes made my mouth water. Evelyn was trying another new Irish recipe. "Hi honey," I said. She sat at the kitchen table with a cup of coffee and a tablet of paper before her. Her head was cradled in her hand as her pencil scratched out her ideas. It reminded me of when she was younger and in school. I saw that pose often. My pride in her spread a smile across my face.

"Hi Mom." She put down her pencil and smiled at me. "Like some coffee? It's fresh. Just made it." She started to get up.

"I'll get it," I said. "I need to start finding my way around here. You can't be waiting on me. I work here too, you know." Evelyn chuckled as I opened a couple of cupboards until I found a cup.

"I can't tell you how much it means to me, Mom, to have you here."

"Well, we'll see if I can live up to your expectations." I smiled over my coffee cup as I sat down across from her.

"You've never failed me yet." She picked up her pencil again and tapped it against the notepad. "I'm sure I'm forgetting something here." She turned the notepad around for me to look at.

I looked over her list of food and supplies and the jobs she'd already checked off. "I can't imagine what it would be. But remember, our bed and breakfast seminar teachers told us that we were sure to make some mistakes and that it was a learning experience. We'll all figure it out together." I patted her hand and gave her back the notepad. "Where's that handsome son-in-law of mine?" I asked as I sipped my coffee.

"He and Finn went over to look at the digs at the castle." A frown crossed her face. "It worries me when they go over there. If someone is upsetting the foundation with their digging, it's not safe."

"I'm sure Charles and Finn will be cautious."

"It just creeps me out a little to know someone has been coming on the property without our seeing him and digging for who knows what." She crossed her arms and rubbed them up and down as if she'd been chilled.

I decided to change the subject. "Those potatoes

smell awfully good. Can I help with anything else for dinner?"

"Thanks, Mom, but I think it's handled. As soon as Charles gets back, he'll set up the grill and do our salmon out there. It shouldn't be long. Finn needs to get home to his wife before she loses her patience and divorces him. He's been spending a lot of long days here."

"About the castle," I said as I set my cup on the table. "Do you have any books here on the history of it? Anything that I might read and something we might pass on to our guests? I'm sure they would be interested."

"I haven't had a chance to look through the library yet but if there is anything to be found, it would be among that collection of books. I've been meaning to spruce that room up. I think we could make it into a very nice reading room or even a music listening room as well if we set up some personal listening devices like they had in the library on the ship. People seemed to enjoy that when they needed a place to relax with their own choice of music."

"What a great idea!" I stood with my empty coffee cup. "Since you don't need me here, why don't I check it out for you and give you some ideas as well as look for a book about the castle."

"Thanks, Mom." Evelyn rose slowly and put her hands on her back bending first one way and then the other.

"You okay?" I asked. It looked like she had winced a bit. "You haven't been lifting more than you should, have you?"

She gave me that look I remembered from when she was little and didn't want to tell me something she'd done. She smiled slightly. "Well, the boxes of linens were a little heavier than I thought but I didn't want you lifting them."

I put my hands on my hips. "Evelyn, we could have managed together. You didn't have to do it by yourself. We're a team, honey. Remember that."

"Yes, Mother," she said petulantly with a coy smile.

I wagged my motherly finger a bit and then went off to find the library. It was tucked into a smaller room behind some double doors in the back of the sitting room or parlor. They really needed to decide what to call that room. A sudden thought crossed my mind from a historical novel set in England I'd just finished. They had morning rooms and withdrawing rooms where they met or entertained guests. I tucked it away for later. Maybe it would serve as an answer for what to call that room.

It was obvious Evelyn had not been in the library yet to do anything with it. It was a bit dusty and musty. I opened up the shutters to let more light in and wiggled a window until I could finally get it to open a bit. Fresh air gushed in as if the old room had taken a deep breath. Hands on hips, I did a full turn in the middle of the room surveying all that was there.

Two large overstuffed green velvet chairs flanked the fireplace at one end of the room. Each had a leather ottoman in front of it and a table with a bronze based lamp on the side. The lampshades looked a bit worn and out of fashion with green tassels hanging around the bottom edge. Bookcases went from floor to ceiling on one wall and were well stocked with hardcover books. There was certainly enough reading material for a houseful of guests. A ladder on wheels that squeaked when I tried to move it allowed someone to get to the uppermost shelves. I would have Charles or Max check out the safety of that ladder before I got on it though.

I perused the lower shelves which contained many old classics and some books of poetry. A section of newer books held volumes of picture books from travel around the world. New and old, they all needed a good dusting. I sneezed several times as I pulled books out to look at them. Finally on a shelf that I could barely reach, I saw a promising book whose title was *Irish Castles*. I stood on tiptoe and pulled the heavy volume out of its spot. It almost fell on my head as I juggled it.

Dust danced in the rays of sunshine from the window as I sat in one of the chairs to page through the book. I guess I shouldn't have been surprised at how many castles were contained in the catalog. After all, Ireland's history was a long one. There was no way I was going to get through all this sitting here before dinner. I decided to take the book to my room where I could spend my evenings looking it over before I went to bed.

One more look at the room and I nodded. Yes, it was a nice room and perfect for reading and listening to relaxing music. Evelyn was right. I was going to get it ship shape as soon as I could. I flinched. My pocket had vibrated again. I dug out my phone.

Made my connection. Boarding for Shannon. Will be there sometime in the morning. Your time of course.

I smiled. I hoped Max could get some sleep on the plane. He'd decided to rent a car at Shannon and drive to Dingle. He'd need to be fresh in the morning to remember which side of the road to drive on. I said a little quick prayer for his safety.

On my way to my room to deposit my book of castles, I met Finn and Charles. They both looked a bit distressed. Charles gave me a smile when he saw me standing there.

"Problems?" I asked as I looked from one to the other.

Charles shook his head in frustration. "More digging at the castle. This time they dislodged one of the larger rocks at the base of a wall and a small part of the wall collapsed sometime last night." He ran a hand through his hair. "One of these mornings we're going to find someone pinned under those rocks."

"Mr. Charles," Finn said turning his cap in circles in his hands. "Whenever you're ready to set up that camera, you let me know. 'Tis a two man job to be done safely."

"Thanks, Finn," Charles said as he placed a hand on the man's shoulder. "Better get yourself home now before Millie locks the door on you."

"Aye," said Finn with a grin at Charles and a nod to me. "Night, Ms. Stengel."

"Casey, Finn. Call me Casey." I smiled at him as his face pinked slightly.

"Miss Casey." Finn nodded again and went on his way. It was a start.

Charles took a deep breath. "Boy, something smells really good."

"It's those roasted potatoes your sweet chef is making." I chuckled and shifted the heavy book of castles in my hands. "I think she's waiting on you to do the salmon. I'll be there to help in a minute. Need to get rid of this." I motioned with the book toward my room.

"Looks like heavy reading."

"It's heavy all right." I grunted as I shifted it from one arm to another. "I wanted to see if I could find some history on this place. I thought it might add interest to our guests' stay."

"Good idea." Charles looked down at his hands. "Guess I'd better get washed up and do my part of the cooking. At least she hasn't taken over my grill." He smiled and went on down the hall.

In my room, I rearranged some things on my nightstand and placed the book there after I gave it a good dusting. I was already thinking of how it might look on a bookstand or coffee table as an item of interest that guests might page through as they sipped tea or coffee in the large sitting room. I felt a little tingle of anticipation. This could turn out to be a lot of fun meeting new people all the time and learning about the places they came from as well as learning more about this place.

I turned to leave. While I was still a bit jet lagged, the smell of food drifting from the kitchen was making my mouth water. I tried to figure out what time my body thought it was and gave up. It didn't matter. I was on Irish time now and with any luck, my body would catch up with it.

4

The quilts and spreads that Evelyn had purchased for the guest rooms were cozy and fit right in with the muted tones of wood paneling and shades of green and blue that accented each room. I put a lighter spread on each bed and folded a heavier quilt at the foot so that guests who needed more warmth could just pull up the quilt and settle in for a comfortable sleep.

As I fluffed the last pillow, I heard two quick beeps of a car horn. That had to be Max. I took a quick check in the mirror of the dresser and patted a few hairs back into place before scurrying out to the front entry just in time to see Charles shake Max's hand and clap him on the back. Finn shook his hand and then Max turned to see me standing there at the door. A big grin stretched across his face and my heart did a little dance.

"There's my girl!" Max said. He took a few long strides toward me and engulfed me in a big warm hug.

When he let go, I feasted my eyes on my wonderful friend. He was wearing his George Clooney look beneath his Dodgers' ball cap. Max had two looks. The George Clooney look that made my heart skip a beat and the Columbo look he used when he was investigating. I'd seen that Columbo look aimed at me a couple of times when we were embroiled in a few mysteries and he needed to ask me questions. I preferred the Clooney look. A light navy jacket covered his broad shoulders and seemed to accent the blue in his eyes. With the late morning sun I had to squint a bit to look up into those deep blue eyes that twinkled despite the weariness of a long flight and a drive on unfamiliar roads on the opposite side of the street he was used to back home.

"How was your drive?" I asked.

"Challenging but once you get the hang of it, not bad. A little harrowing when you're making turns but I kept reminding myself to stay to the left." He laughed. "There was also a polite reminder on the dashboard of the rental car." Max put an arm around me and we turned to Charles and Finn who were sporting sly smiles.

"So," Max said, "where do I start?"

"Why don't you get settled and then you can join Finn and me in deciding how to set up a trail camera for security at the castle. It just got delivered this morning," Charles said. "Unless of course you'd like a little time to catch up with Casey." He winked at Max.

Max looked at me and smiled then, then as if a switch had gone off in his head, he whipped around again to Charles. "Security camera? At the castle? What is there to protect over there?" Max nodded in the direction of the partially collapsed walls. "Doesn't look like anything valuable could possibly be there."

"That's just it. We don't know why but someone keeps going over there at night and digging holes. They've already collapsed part of another wall." Charles shook his head. "Whether there's anything valuable or not, we need to keep a watch. Our property owners are very conscious of liability issues and we certainly can't afford someone getting hurt over there even if they've brought it on themselves."

"You boys go ahead and get on with your work," I said. "I have my own to finish. Max and I can catch up later after dinner." I laughed. "That is if he's still awake when the jet lag hits him."

Max stiffened a bit. "I'll be fine," he said quite seriously. "I've spent many a night working straight through on investigations and learned how to get on without a lot of sleep." He made me feel a bit chastised but

I brushed it off as the effects of jet lag whether or not he wanted to fess up to it.

Charles helped Max get his bags from the car and as I followed them back into the lodge I couldn't help but wonder if Max was already missing his job at the sheriff's office. After thirty years of homicide investigations, he decided it was time to retire. I think you can take the man out of the job but it takes a while to get the job out of the man. He had immediately inquired about the security camera and the reason for it, already tuning in to the possibility of a crime or at least a mystery to solve. How would he take to this new life in a new country? A new job so completely different from what he had done for so many years? At least he won't have to deal with the horrible crimes that had left him a bit skeptical of people and in many ways ever so suspicious. Hopefully he would get over that. And perhaps having a little mystery at the castle would give him a chance to use his investigative skills while he adjusted to all the new things in his life.

The afternoon passed quickly. Charles took Max around the lodge and the grounds before lunch and pointed out some of the things that needed repair as well as plans for improvement. Evelyn had a lovely lunch laid out of sandwiches and soup and as soon as we finished eating, the men headed out to the castle to work on installing the trail camera. Evelyn and I cleaned up the dishes and decided to start on sprucing up the library. Charles and Max had checked out the library's ladder on their tour around the lodge and deemed it safe enough although there were lots of warnings about being careful climbing up and down. Charles promised to return later with some oil for the squeaky wheels.

We stood at the door and surveyed the room. "Where shall we start?" I asked.

"How about we tackle the biggest job first?" said Evelyn. "We'll start at the top of the bookcases and work our way down. Let's take all of the books off the shelves and see what we want to keep and what we can get rid of."

"Are you thinking of keeping the upper shelves empty?" I imagined guests climbing to the top of the ladder to see what was on the highest shelves.

"In the interest of safety, yes." Evelyn nodded her head and pointed to the topmost shelves. "I just don't think we need to tempt any guests to see what's up there. One or two rungs on the ladder, maybe three, are fine but any higher and I'd be nervous about someone falling."

The bookcases lined the long wall of one side of the library across from the windows. Between the windows were several cabinets. As I looked around again, an idea began to form. "Evelyn, what if we were to empty the top shelves but instead of just leaving them to collect dust and cobwebs we could have Max install wood panels that are painted to look like books. We would have to be sure guests knew they were fake so they wouldn't climb up to look at them but it would keep the look of a full library as well as cut down on the cleaning."

"Great idea, Mom!" Evelyn hugged me. "Do you think Max will do it?"

"That's what you hired him for, right? Light construction?" I said with a smile. "Let's get started here."

We grabbed the utility cart from the supply room and another smaller ladder. Evelyn climbed to the top of the tall wheeled ladder and handed books down to me as I stood on the smaller one. I placed as many as I could on the cart and then wheeled it over to a large folding table we'd set up to sort the books. It didn't take long before the table was full and I was stashing books underneath it.

"That's a lot of books," I said when we'd finally cleaned out the top two shelves. "Will the owners want them put in storage?" I stood looking at the pile with my hands on my hips and took a deep breath.

"I have permission to do what I want with the lodge contents, within reason of course. So we'll put the ones in really bad condition in one pile, the ones that look like they might be valuable like a first edition or a really old edition in another pile, and the ones that look like someone might actually read in another." Evelyn said picking up a few and looking them over. "What do you think?"

"Sounds like a good plan. What are we going to do with the ones we don't want?"

"I'll ask Finn's wife. I think she has some connection to the library in Dingle and perhaps they'll want some of them or at least be able to tell us what we can pitch that have no value. Our donation could create some good will with the community as well." Evelyn looked at her watch and then glanced around the room again. "I'm sorry to leave you with this but I need to respond to some people who have inquired about booking rooms. Our website is live now and we're beginning to generate interest." She smiled but I could see the little tic at the corner of her mouth that told me she was a bit anxious about diving into this new venture.

"When do you think we'll have our first guests?" I asked as my stomach did a little flutter at the thought. I wouldn't admit it to Evelyn but I was a bit nervous as well about this whole new adventure.

"Well, you've got half the guest rooms in great shape already and the rest of the lodge is looking good. Millie, Finn's wife, is going to join our crew tomorrow and she can help us with the finishing touches." Evelyn touched the spot where I knew her butterflies were fluttering. "If we don't get the library done before the first one arrives, we can always close the doors." She waved a hand over our pile of books. "Maybe a few of these could go in the gathering room for guests to look through."

"Gathering room?" I smiled. "So you've decided to call it that?"

"I kicked around some ideas that were old English terms for rooms like morning room or withdrawing room. I've read a few Victorian novels that used those terms but they just didn't seem to fit here. I like gathering room. It implies a place that brings people together."

"Perfect," I said, realizing that our tastes in reading seemed to be the same. "You run along. I'll dig into our pile of books here unless you have something else that you need me to do. If Millie helps out tomorrow, we can finish up the rest of the guest rooms quickly."

"Okay." Evelyn took a deep breath. "I'm off to confirm our first guests. Wish me luck."

I gave her a little hug. "Honey, you don't need luck. You're doing a great job."

With a deep breath, I turned to the pile of books. This was the beginning of what I was sure would be quite a lot of work but it might offer some more information about the castle and the lodge. Who knew what kind of treasure might be revealed between the old dusty book covers?

I got into a bit of a rhythm with setting books in the appropriate piles. I'd found a couple that were either first editions or very early editions and then I picked up a book that was titled *The Case Of The Irish Crown Jewels*. It caught my interest and I leafed through a few pages. The book was about a theft of the crown jewels of Ireland. I figured it was a mystery novel and might prove entertaining when I needed to relax with a good book. I started a new pile. My own pile of books to read. I was sure I'd find more.

Max stuck his head in the door and gave a low whistle. "So this is where you've been hiding out all afternoon." He strode over to a pile of old books and picked one up. "This looks like it's been well read or else it's just deteriorating from old age."

"I'd rather think it was well loved," I said taking the book from him and replacing it on the pile he pulled it from. "I hate to think of anything or anyone deteriorating from old age."

He smiled at me. "Well, I was sent in to see if you'd like to join in on afternoon tea."

"Afternoon tea? I thought that was something you only did in England."

"Apparently your daughter says it's still a tradition in Ireland as well and something she wanted to try out." He shrugged a bit. "I guess we're the test group."

"Sounds like the kind of test group I could enjoy." I locked my arm in his. "Let's go, Sir Lancelot."

He gave me a strange look. "Lancelot?"

"You know. Sir Lancelot. Lady Guinevere. Knights of the Round Table. King Arthur."

"Wasn't that English lore?" He said as we walked out into the gathering room.

"Hmmm. You're right. Guess I'd better check on my Irish lore and folk tales before I embarrass myself in front of any Irish guests."

Evelyn had set up a sideboard in the dining room with teapots of hot water and a selection of tea bags. Plates of delicate pastries, small bite sized sandwiches and little biscuits she called scones sat on an embroidered linen table runner. Charles and Finn had already filled their small plates with goodies and were sipping their tea.

"The scones are perfect, Miss Evelyn," Finn said as he smoothed whipped cream and strawberry jam over another half scone.

"Even without the clotted cream?" Evelyn asked.

"Oh yes. The whipped cream is a good substitute when you can't get the real stuff." Finn stuffed another bite into his mouth and his face showed his enjoyment.

Max and I joined the others at the table and I eagerly spread my scone with cream and jam and savored my first bite. Along with the rest of the offerings, I could see where afternoon tea could become a favorite. Hopefully once the guests arrived, we would get to enjoy it as well.

"Say, Finn," Max said as he frowned at a little cucumber sandwich before he popped the whole thing into his mouth. "Casey expressed an interest in learning a little more about some Irish lore and folk tales. Maybe you could tell her that story you told us over at the castle." The cucumber sandwich must have been to his liking because he reached for the one on my plate and with a lopsided grin snatched it away.

"Sure," said Finn. He took another sip of his tea and cleared his throat. "I suppose it qualifies as folk lore not a fairy tale because there is some truth to it. Back in 1907 the crown jewels of Ireland were stolen. Now there wasn't really a crown. It was a collection of jewels that belonged to the Order of St. Patrick. They were kept in a bank vault but a few years before the theft, they were moved to a safe in the library of the Dublin Castle.

"At the time the keeper of the keys was a Sir Arthur Vicars. It seems there were two keys and one he kept with him all the time. The second key somehow got misplaced and was found by a maid to be on a key ring containing many other keys. It was shortly after that the theft was discovered."

"Did they ever find the jewels or who did it?" I asked.

"Not exactly," Finn said rubbing his trim red beard and pausing. He was a good storyteller. "Vicars was blamed mostly for his negligence and he was removed from his position. He insisted that the culprit was one of his heralds, Francis Shackleton."

"Shackleton?" I was surprised at the name. "Wasn't he the famous Antarctic explorer? I remember reading a book about him."

"That would be Ernest his brother. Francis was a bit of a rogue. Got himself into trouble often, was even in prison once or twice." Finn paused again obviously delighting in the telling of his tale. "He disappeared around 1915 and the jewels were never found."

Max folded his hands on the table in front of him and leaned in as if there were a conspiracy. "Tell her the connection to Shamrock." He leaned back again and gave me his Columbo look.

"Ah yes," Finn said with a slightly crooked smile. "The connection. Well the story goes, Shackleton was a friend to Sir Muir who owned Castle Glas, the name given originally to Castle Shamrock. The local people like to tell stories of great parties at the Castle and the tale is told of some relatives who swear they saw Shackleton there."

"That would be a great story to tell our guests," I said to Evelyn. "Maybe we could collect a few more and write them all down in a little pamphlet or something."

"Mom, right now I don't think there is one more thing I can put on my list," Evelyn said with a tired smile. "Maybe later."

"I'll take that on as my job but you're right. Later rather than sooner. We do have a lot to do." I stood. "And I guess I'd better get back to it." With that everyone rose and took their cups and plates to place on the tray that Evelyn had set out to collect the used china and silver.

I felt a hand on my arm as I started to leave. "So what did you think about afternoon tea?" Evelyn asked. "Should we make it a routine?"

"Perfect. Absolutely perfect and if you think you can handle the extra work then, yes, it should be an offering to our guests." I patted the hand on my arm. "Thanks, honey, for including me in your decisions."

Evelyn smiled. "We're all in this together." She looked around at the remnants of the afternoon treats. "I think with Millie's help, I can manage a daily tea." She looked at me again and the smile widened. "It'll be fun." She grabbed the tray of used dishes and headed for the kitchen.

As I walked through the gathering room to the library, I thought about all the hard work we'd done and what was ahead. In a way it was kind of fun. The best part was doing it all together.

5

Millie, Finn's wife, sparkled like a real gem. Her face shone with a radiant happiness as if she were a new bride. Those lovely emerald green eyes of hers were the first thing that drew me in. Her hair was more brown rather than the red of her husband Finn's and the fresh rush of excitement she brought to our work-weary and nervous bunch was just what was needed. She was dressed in a pair of jeans and a light blue cotton button-down shirt with sleeves rolled up to the elbows. Her bright pink Nikes matched her bright personality.

"Well, now," she said in a voice that was lovely and delicate yet full of confidence, "catch me up on what you've done and where I can get started." We were all gathered in the kitchen finishing up breakfast when Finn and Millie arrived. Evelyn invited them to join us for a cup of coffee, or rather the tea that they preferred, and a breakfast roll while we talked about our day ahead. Charles was off to do some troubleshooting with his security camera system. Max had found some wood trim on the house that needed replacing and he and Finn were off to the lumber yard to get supplies. Evelyn would take Millie to see the prepared guest rooms and explain what our routine would be. We had decided that I would do the light cleaning and refreshing of the guest rooms while Millie helped Evelyn with serving breakfast. Then Millie and I would do the more detailed cleaning of rooms later in the day when we needed to prepare rooms for new guests or swap out the used linens for fresh. It all sounded good when we planned it. I hoped it would work well.

I set off to work some more in the library. I hoped we could get it up and ready soon. It would be such a wonderful space for our guests especially those who were here to relax and enjoy the countryside and the ocean. Max had said that he could make some fake fronts for the top shelves of the library but he was no artist. There was no way he was going to paint them to look like books. Evelyn thought she might have an idea for that though. She had been to a town festival and remembered a clever artist who was a local and thought he might like the job. I still needed to get the rest of the shelves cleared of books and then dusted before we rearranged them and put them back.

"Would you be wantin' a little help here?" Millie asked, surprising me enough while I was coming down the ladder that I dropped a book. "Oh! Sorry, dinna mean to startle you so." She hurried over and picked up the book then reached for the others I had.

"No harm done," I said as I handed her the other books and carefully made my way down the last couple of rungs. "Guess I was just concentrating too hard on what I was doing to hear you come in."

Millie turned slowly to survey the room. "This is a beautiful room." She lifted the books in her hands slightly. "And full of treasures."

"You enjoy reading?" I asked as I took the books from her and set them on the pile to be sorted.

"Oh yes," Millie said, her green eyes brightening. She walked over to the table with the sorted books and began to run her fingers lightly over them. "I love how they take you to places you've never been and show you things you might never see yourself. They are each an adventure, a way to explore and to learn."

"What a wonderful thing to say." I turned back to the ladder and started to climb. Millie put a hand on my arm before I got to the second rung.

"You let me be climbin'," she said. "You've been up and down enough already. Let me share the work."

I moved aside and she was up to the shelf I was emptying before I could say anything more. Eager to help. Enthusiastic. And she loved books too. I was going to like having Millie around. We worked until lunchtime and took a break with the others to enjoy a ploughman's sandwich of pastrami, cheese, tomatoes, onions, salad greens and mustard all on homemade potato bread that Millie had brought with her. I had to admire Evelyn for her research on different Irish foods and traditions and Millie for all the hard work she did. While working in the library she had told me of volunteering at the town library and the local hospital.

When we finished sorting through books, I found the empty boxes that had held our new linens and other household items and we filled them with the books for the town library donation. They were too heavy for us to lift so Millie went to see if the men were free to load them into Finn's truck. Allie came into the library carrying an old tennis ball. She dropped it on the floor in front of me, hunched down and then sprang up as if she wanted to run.

"Okay girl," I said. "I recognize cabin fever when I see it." I picked up the ball and her ears perked. Her tail went into high gear as it wagged. She started turning circles, dancing in front of me. I laughed. "Let's go outside so we don't cause any trouble in here." She knew exactly what I meant and beat me to the front door where she sat impatiently waiting, her bottom barely touching the floor and her tail sweeping back and forth.

Outside, I led her to an open grassy area and tossed the ball. She eagerly retrieved it and dropped it at my feet. We did that several times, each time I tossed it a little farther. It gave me time to take in the fresh air and the sunshine of a perfect day. I could smell the sea air as the wind carried it up from the harbor. I noticed that Finn had started on an area that Evelyn hoped would be a garden from which she could get fresh vegetables and herbs for cooking.

Allie bounded toward me again, ready for another toss of the ball. This time she teased me with it before she finally let go and I could give it a good toss. She took off running and caught up with it as it bounced but she stopped after picking up the ball and looked out into the distance. A large flock of gulls had landed by the castle. Allie dropped the ball and bounded across the grass in the direction of the castle and the gulls.

"Allie! Allie!" I called. She never hesitated. The herding instinct had taken over and she was going to round up those gulls. How she expected to do that when they were just going to fly off was beyond me but I was concerned she would continue to chase after them and I wouldn't get her back. I hustled as fast as I could over the rough terrain of tufted grass to catch up with her. By the time I was near, she had already chased off the gulls and was sniffing the ground as if to wonder where they'd gone.

Just as I was about to catch up with her, she started running again but this time she stopped every few yards to sniff the ground again. I took a moment to pause and catch my breath. Was this dog part bloodhound as well as border collie? She seemed to be on the trail of something.

My heart sunk as she disappeared around the end wall of the castle. "Allie! Allie!" Like an insistent teenager bent on proclaiming her own independence, she ignored me. My pulse quickened as I rounded the wall and looked for her. She was stopped and sniffing all around a pile of rocks that had obviously collapsed from the wall. While I was nervous about getting too close to the wall, I knew I needed to get close enough to her to grab her collar and lead her back home.

I crept forward carefully, hoping I didn't spook her into running again. "What do you have there, girl?" She lifted her head for a moment to look at me then lowered it again. She was intent on what she had found and kept excitedly sniffing around the rocks. "Gotcha!" I said as I reached down and hooked my fingers through her collar. She looked up at me with great big eyes as if trying to tell me something then pulled my arm down as her nose went to the pile of rocks again.

"What is it, girl?" She was whining now. I looked closer and realized there was a hand poking out from between two rocks. A wave of dizziness came over me as I realized someone was buried under all those rocks. Was he still alive? Was it one of our men? They hadn't talked of working over here today. My stomach churned and my pulse raced. Still holding Allie with one hand, I reached down and touched the hand that was there. Cold. Very cold. I doubted with all the weight upon him he could possibly be anything but dead. A check of his wrist indicated no pulse.

"Allie, be a good girl," I said looking at her as she tried to wiggle free from me. I managed to pull my cell phone from my pocket. Thank goodness Charles had gotten me local service on a new phone. I tapped his number on my contact list.

"Casey! Trying out the new phone?" Charles laughed as he answered.

"N-no," my voice was a bit shaky, "I-I found s-something at the castle. You better come."

6

All three men came. I guess I must have scared Charles with what I'd said. Allie was a little calmer. I removed my belt and hooked it around her collar. She was behaving very nicely thank goodness. I gave an apologetic smile to the men as they arrived but I could feel my mouth quiver. I knew what was coming and as soon as I pointed to the pile of rocks and they saw what was there, it came.

Max turned to me. "Well, you've done it again, Schweetheart," he said putting an arm around me. My eyes widened. I knew Max had a Clooney and Columbo side. It was Clooney when he was charming and romantic. The Columbo side, one eyebrow raised, squinting and hair tousled, came through when he was investigating. Now I feared I needed to add a Bogart side too. "How did you find this body?"

Charles and Finn stood one on each side of Max, the same question obviously on their faces. I shook my head. "I didn't find this one." I looked down at Allie who seemed to be quite pleased with herself. Her ears were perked and her tail wagged. "Allie did." I explained what had happened. "I checked. There was no pulse."

Charles stepped forward and gave me a hug. "Still had to be a shock. I'm sorry you were the one she brought here." Keeping one arm around me, he turned to Max who was now bent over the pile of rocks. "Max, should we try to dig him out?"

"Absolutely not," Max said looking back to the pile of rocks and the contents it held. "The local authorities need to work on that. We don't want to disturb any evidence of what happened here."

"Already alerted them," Finn said sliding his cell phone back into his pocket. "Do you s'pose he might be our digger? Could'o dislodged the wrong rock that was holding up that part of the wall."

In the distance I could hear the sing-song whoop of a siren. It sounded a bit different from the ones back home. Allie got a little too excited again and started straining at the makeshift leash. "I'd better get Allie home," I said. "I'll let Evelyn know what's going on as well. If anyone needs me, I'll be in the kitchen with a big cup of coffee, calming my nerves." I saw that Max already had his Columbo persona in place. He was down on one knee studying the pile of rocks and the wall they had fallen from. It didn't take much to reengage old habits. It would have been nice though had he at least taken notice that I was leaving.

"Thanks, Casey," Charles said. "Tell Ev we'll be there as soon as we can."

Once inside the lodge, Allie made a mad dash for her water dish. I guess discovering a body made her thirsty. It just made me anxious. I'd been this route before and I wasn't looking forward to all the questions and all the investigating. At least this time I wasn't quite so intimately involved and I doubted I could be suspect.

While Allie retreated to her comfy dog bed and promptly fell asleep, Evelyn, Millie and I sat around the kitchen table. None of us was ready to dig back into the work that needed done. Maybe dig was the wrong word to use. The guys would be helping the local authorities dig out the body and try to discover if he was responsible for making the holes near the castle walls.

Millie refilled our coffee cups and poured herself more tea. "We haven't had a mysterious death here since they found the owner of the lodge murdered some years back." She returned the coffee pot to the counter.

Evelyn and I shared a wide-eyed look. "Murdered? In the lodge?" I swallowed hard.

Millie sat down. "Yes. 'Twas a frightful thing. They never discovered who did it or why. Left the whole town a bit uneasy." She blew across her teacup. "The couple who bought the lodge cleaned it up and tried to refresh the furnishings so that it wouldn't be a reminder but they were always uneasy about living here. Strange noises in the night. Felt they were being watched and intruded upon. They changed the locks but the uneasiness continued. They finally put the lodge on the market and that's when your company bought it."

"Could there be a connection?" I wondered aloud. I looked at Evelyn. "Our owner company never said a thing about a murder. Did they know? Is that really why they want the security cameras set up?" I shuddered. "None of us have heard strange noises in the night and except for the digging at the castle, I don't feel we were being watched. Were we?" I looked at Evelyn.

"Good question," Evelyn said. "It all makes a little more sense for setting up the security cameras rather than just a liability issue. Guess we'll have to inquire about what they knew when we tell them of this new development." Evelyn rose with her empty cup in hand. "I need to get something started for dinner. Who knows when the guys will be done out there. Any suggestions?"

"How about we all go into town to the Fungie?" Millie put her teacup down and smiled at the look of confusion on our faces. "They've got great collar and cabbage. And of course Guinness on tap."

"Great idea," said Evelyn rising from her chair. "I'll finish up with my responses to reservation inquiries and get a shower. Hopefully the men won't be too long."

"A shower sounds good but I think I'd better keep myself available for questions from the police. Unfortunately I'm all too familiar with how these investigations go." I rose with my coffee cup in hand.

"Millie, if you'll tidy up the kitchen, I'll work a bit more in that library."

"I'll join you when I'm done. Finn has the boxed books in the back of the truck. We can drop them at the library when it opens in the morning. Guess we just need to decide how we want to organize what's left."

Before we could get back to work, Charles and Finn came in with the local police chief. He greeted us with an apology for this unfortunate incident and wanted us to understand that this was a very unusual occurrence. "The young lad you found is not from this area. He has some identification on him that indicates he is a student at University College Dublin. We'll have someone look up his family and try to establish just what he was doin' here at the castle."

"Do you suppose he was the one making all the holes at the castle?" I asked looking from the police chief to Charles.

"It's hard to say but I think it's likely. I wish I could have gotten that camera working properly sooner. Then we'd know for sure." Charles pointed to the kitchen table. "Chief, how about a cup of tea or coffee while you interview Casey?"

"Tea would be good. Thanks."

Charles turned to Millie who was at the sink. She nodded to him. "I'll wet the tea. Won't take but a moment." She filled the kettle and placed it on the stove.

The chief pulled out a chair for me and invited me to sit. "Casey is it?" He pulled out a notebook much like the one Max carried. "Can you give me your full name?"

"Kathleen Catherine O'Shaughnessy Stengel." The chief raised an eyebrow when he had finished writing all of that. "You can see why I prefer Casey Stengel," I said feeling myself blush.

"Casey Stengel." He nodded. "Wasn't that one of your famous ball players?"

My smile widened almost into a grin. It was nice to meet someone in Ireland who knew about the legendary

Stengel. “Yes,” I said. “I guess that’s why I’m a big baseball fan.”

“Ah,” he nodded his head. “You’re gonna have to try one of our cricket matches. I’m sure you’ll love it.”

The chief drank his tea and asked his questions about how I’d found the body. There really wasn’t much to tell but he drew it out enough to enjoy his cup of tea and Millie’s cookies, or rather biscuits as I learned they were called. He thanked us and excused himself, promising to tell us if he discovered anything about the unfortunate young man I’d found.

Max came in just as the chief was leaving. “Chief,” he said reaching out with a piece of paper that was smudged with soil. “I found this while we were moving a few more rocks to get that young man out.” He handed the paper to the chief. “It looks like a diagram of the castle walls. I’m guessing he’s our digger but heaven knows what he was digging for.”

As Max was talking with the chief, I recalled what Finn had said about Shamrock, Francis Shackleton and the stolen Irish crown jewels. Could there be a connection?

When the Chief and his men were gone, we all hurried to clean up a bit and then four of us in Evelyn’s van followed Millie and Finn in his truck into town to the Fungie pub. It was a rustic sort of place near the water’s edge. The building was mostly a gray stone that here and there had some green moss growing on it. The entrance was a polished dark wood that, to my housekeeping eye, must have required a lot of work to keep up. Inside, thick timbers stretched across a ceiling of smooth planked boards in warm mahogany colors. Tables and chairs shone with a polish of loving care and use.

Once inside, we discovered the reason for its name. The menu told the story. In the harbor was a bottle-nosed dolphin who had adopted the town as its home and for the last thirty plus years had entertained locals and visitors alike with its friendly shenanigans meeting boats in the harbor and interacting with the passengers. We were encouraged to find some time to take a boat ride out into the harbor and meet him.

Max was not sure he would like boiled bacon with cabbage so he passed on the special collar and cabbage and opted for the shepherd's pie. The rest of us ordered the house specialty and of course we all wanted a Guinness. The Guinness was an unusual ale. It had a foamy top that was almost creamy. The deep brown ale was a bit strong for me but at least I could say I'd been to Ireland and had a Guinness.

When our dinners came, Max tasted my collar and cabbage then ate half of it. He offered me half his shepherd's pie in return. I turned down the pie. The pint of Guinness had quite filled me up. I did taste his pie though and it was every bit as good as my bacon and cabbage which turned out to be more like pork belly.

As we sat finishing our pints of Guinness, Max pulled out his cell phone and opened up a picture. He handed the phone to Charles. "Before I gave that paper to the Chief, I took a picture of it. Thought we might get an idea of what the fellow was doing over there."

Charles and Finn bent their heads over the phone and Charles manipulated the picture to be able to see better. "Did you figure out where the body was on the diagram?"

"Best as I can tell," Max said setting his empty beer mug on the table, "it was there by that place marked dovecote. Whatever that is."

I saw Finn smile at Millie. "A dovecote," Millie began, "is a place in a castle where pigeons or doves were kept."

"Homing pigeons?" I wasn't sure when the idea of using homing pigeons had begun but I was sure it was a long time ago.

"No, no," Millie continued, "not homing pigeons. The doves and pigeons were kept as a food source. The eggs were quite good and of course roast pigeon was a staple. And then there was always plenty of dung for fertilizing the garden."

I think Millie was amused by the looks on our faces. We modern Americans were quite surprised at, what to us, seemed a disgusting source of food. I'm sure we were all thinking about the awful pigeons we'd encountered in large cities. They seemed to be very dirty creatures and not the least bit appetizing but maybe we could reduce the population if we started eating them. I shuddered at the thought.

Evelyn laughed. "Well, I don't think that's something I'll put on the menu."

Max seemed to be the only one who wasn't amused. I could see that Columbo look on his face or was it Bogart? No definitely Columbo. He was mulling over ideas of what might have happened at the castle to contribute to a dead body being found.

"The dovecote might have been an excellent place to hide something of value." Max took a last sip of his Guinness. "Think about it. It would not be a pleasant place to enter with all of those birds fluttering around and of course all the dung. It must have smelled awful. A person wouldn't want to spend more time in there than necessary." He pushed his empty beer mug to the center of the table and leaned forward. "And what a perfectly good alarm system. Birds squawking and fluttering and creating a racket anytime someone entered the place."

We all sat silently for a moment contemplating what Max had said. Slowly Charles began to nod his head. "You might have something, Max. But what in the world would be valuable enough for someone to risk his life digging in an unstable castle where walls are crumbling?"

"The Irish crown jewels," I blurted out. All eyes turned to me. From their expressions, I felt like an umpire who had just called a ball a strike. Unlike an umpire, I felt I had to defend my comment. "Finn, didn't you tell us the story of the theft of the crown jewels? You said Shackleton was connected somehow to the theft and to the castle. Could he have brought them here and buried them in the dovecote?"

Finn dipped his head down and studied his empty beer mug. I could tell he was hiding a smile. When he looked up at me again, he was composed. "Miss Casey, the theft of the jewels has turned into more folk lore and tales than fact. I just shared it because you wanted to learn a bit more about Irish folk lore. I canna believe the jewels would be buried here."

Max looked at Finn. "There were real jewels, right?"

Finn nodded. "For sure. The tellin' of that is true."

"Shackleton was implicated in the theft was he not?" Finn nodded again. "And he had some connection to the castle, correct?"

"As the story goes," Finn said. He looked at Millie and she shrugged and he turned to Max again. "After all this time? Only a fool would believe there were jewels buried there."

"A fool who might get himself killed looking for them?" Max let the question hang in the air.

7

It was Friday. Our first guest was due to arrive. I couldn't decide if we were all just nervous or too excited. There was certainly the feel of electricity in the air that seemed to charge all of us with a new anticipation of the unknown. Were we ready? Could we do this? I took a deep breath before I poured myself a cup of coffee and sat down with my toast and the homemade jam Evelyn had purchased from one of the locals at the market in town. We would be doing our own jam when the berries began coming in later in the spring and summer.

I looked around the table at the others. Max was scooping up the rest of his eggs with his toast and Charles poked around in his oatmeal, deep in thought. Evelyn sat down beside me with her coffee just as Millie and Finn arrived. We all looked up at them as they approached the table.

"Top of the mornin' to you," Finn said cheerfully.

"And the rest of the day to you," said Charles. He grinned. "Did I get it right?"

"Perfect." Finn pulled out a chair while Millie poured hot water into the teapot from the kettle that Evelyn had heated to make tea for the two of them as they preferred tea to coffee. "Important day today, yes?"

"Yes," said Evelyn with a deep sigh. "I hope we're ready for this. I keep going over everything. I'm sure there's something I've missed."

I reached out my hand and patted hers. "Honey, all the bases are covered. If there's an error somewhere, we'll make up for it and hit it out of the ballpark."

Charles chuckled. "Casey, I take it you were able to play back that ballgame I recorded for you?" He raised an eyebrow as the gold flecks in his dark brown eyes twinkled with humor. "Your baseball analogies are back."

"Oh," I said with surprise. "I didn't know I was doing that." I looked at Max who smiled at me across his coffee cup. "Max and I watched it together but one of us couldn't keep our eyes open." Actually, it had been a very pleasant evening as we sat on the small sofa in my room and held hands while we watched our beloved Dodgers pull ahead of the Padres. I thought perhaps Max was content with their lead and that's why he was relaxed enough to fall asleep. I enjoyed listening to his steady breathing.

"Okay, okay. I'll admit it." Max set his cup down. "I haven't done this much physical activity in a while. I must be getting old. It wears me out."

"I've appreciated every minute you've given me," said Charles smiling broadly. He reached for another mini muffin Evelyn had made to accompany the eggs and sausage and toast for breakfast. "As good as Finn is, we couldn't have done all this work without an extra pair of hands."

"Aye," said Finn nodding his head. He raised his teacup in a salute to Max. "Fer an old man, you work pretty good." He flashed a crooked grin at Max. I was glad to see Max respond with a smile. It appeared that the three men were all getting along well together.

"Is there any news on our poor boy who got buried beneath the rocks?" Millie asked. She must have gotten a bit of sun the day before helping Finn in the gardens. Her rosy cheeks brightened her fair skin. Millie's brown curly hair was tied back with a blue tri-cornered scarf but small tendrils had escaped and framed her pretty freckled face. She sipped her tea as she looked from Charles to Max.

Charles swallowed the last of the mini muffin he'd popped in his mouth. "The chief stopped by and said they had found the boy's parents. He was an international student from New York studying Irish folklore. It seems their ancestry traces back to Ireland. They will arrange to ship his body home for services there." Charles shook his head. "So young. So sad. What could he possibly have been doing there at the castle?"

Max cleared his throat. "I'd place my bet on digging for treasure. There had to be a reason he had that diagram of the castle with him. I hope we can get the trail camera up and working properly today just in case there's more than one treasure hunter. At least we can keep an eye on any activity there."

Charles pushed his chair back. "Well then, we'd better get started." He looked at Evelyn. "Unless you have something pressing that needs our attention in the lodge?"

Evelyn shook her head. "Nope. I think all the major repairs are done and all we have left is to make sure it's all clean and then finish off that library. I think Mom and Millie can handle that and I'll make the preparations in the kitchen for our Friday night dinner. I'm going to make that Irish stew you all liked. Hope our guest will too."

As Millie and I started for the library, I wondered if Evelyn's plans for the bed and breakfast weren't a little too ambitious. Providing breakfast every morning for guests was one thing and then the afternoon tea but she had decided every Friday there would be a traditional Irish meal at dinner time as well. That was putting a lot of pressure on a girl who wasn't even Irish.

The shutters were closed and the library looked a bit dreary without the morning light streaming in. I looked at Millie, "I'll get those shutters opened and try the windows again now that the men have made them easier to open. A little fresh air and sunshine will do wonders in here."

"Aye," said Millie. "I'm wonderin' if I should open the windows in our guest's bedroom. It will be much fresher with the cool air comin' in."

"Good idea. I'll start dusting here too so we can put these books all back on the shelves now that we've decided where they are going."

Millie left me to the shutters, the windows, and to begin the dusting. Once the sun was coming in as well as the fresh air, it made the chore of dusting seem lighter. I had a long handled rod that had a great disposable dust catcher on the end of it which was easily replaced with a clean one. Considering how long it had been since these shelves were cleaned, I expected to go through a couple of replacement dust catchers.

Even though the handle was long and I could adjust it to an angle to make it easier to reach some spots, I still needed to climb the ladder a bit to reach the top shelf. Max had cut the wood for the fake books that would fill the top two shelves and the artist in town now had them and was working on them. He hoped to have them done in a day or so for Max to install. I carefully moved the ladder to the shelves nearest the corner windows that flanked the fireplace. Max and Finn had cleaned out the fireplace and set it with wood in case the weather turned on us and it would feel good to have the warm glow of a fire. I started up the ladder carefully.

When I got far enough to reach the top shelf, I wrapped an arm around the ladder and used my other hand to manipulate the duster. A shower of dust came from the back of the shelf which gave me a fit of sneezing. I fumbled in my pocket for a tissue and blew my nose as I promised myself to be more careful to push the dust off the side instead of directly in front of me. I made a couple more swoops of the duster and suddenly felt it stop against something in the corner. Had we missed a book? I pushed harder with the duster and felt something budge. A little more finagling and I was able to maneuver the object closer to the edge. I was afraid to climb much higher so I pushed just a bit more to the edge hoping to see what it might be and if I could reach it.

Without warning, a packet of papers flew off the shelf and fell to the floor. I almost lost my balance as my first instinct was to reach out to catch it. I looked down as the packet of papers hit the wooden floor at the edge of the rug and watched the rubber band break scattering the papers that it had held together. I climbed down carefully and gathered the folded pages together. Were they letters? Someone's notes from a book?

I unfolded the first and realized it was a letter. The handwriting was a bit hard to read. I moved closer to the light coming in the window but it didn't help. There wasn't time for this now. I folded it up and stacked the papers together again. There was a clean cloth in my supply basket where I kept cleaning supplies handy. I wrapped the letters in it so they wouldn't be soiled by anything and tucked them into my basket.

By the time Millie returned, I had finished one bookcase, replaced my duster, and was dusting off a beautiful piece of artwork that hung on the paneled section between the bookcases. The picture was of a castle and was painted on glass in such a way that it almost looked like a stained-glass window. There were bits of gold leaf that accented some of the castle's turrets and windows. When the overhead light was turned on and spotlighted it, the picture gleamed and sparkled. I wondered if it was Shamrock Castle. I still hadn't found a picture of what the castle looked like before walls began to fall.

Millie stood, hands on her hips as she watched me climb down again from the ladder and take a deep breath. "Sure, would you like me to do a bit of the climbin'?" She asked with a smile.

"I wouldn't object to a little rest," I said as I rubbed my calves that felt sore as I flexed them. "Guess I'm old and out of shape."

"No," said Millie as she positioned the ladder in front of the next set of bookcases. She reached for the duster in my hand. "I'll be just as sore as you when we're done." I doubted that but I gratefully handed her the duster.

We worked, dusting and polishing the furniture and replacing the books until lunch. The two of us stood with arms around each other admiring our work. "It's beautiful," I said. "All we need are those fake book panels installed and it'll be finished. Well, finished until Evelyn decides to add her music to it."

"Music?" Millie picked up a bundle of cleaning cloths that were soiled. "Will she have musicians play?"

"No, I don't believe so but that sounds like a lovely idea. She's planning on having individual listening devices for those who might like to listen quietly to their own choice of music as they read. They had them on the cruise ship where she worked and the guests seemed to enjoy them." I picked up my basket of supplies and we left to see what Evelyn had planned for lunch. I had to admit, I'd worked up an appetite.

Everyone gathered around the kitchen table for corned beef sandwiches with pickles. Allie sat impatiently waiting for something, anything to drop for her to retrieve. She was beginning to have a little self control but just barely. Evelyn had a plate of fresh sliced vegetables to munch on as well and there was iced tea for the Americans in the group and hot tea for the Irish who had tried the cold brew and found it not to their liking. "I don't know how you can drink hot tea on a warm day," Max said as he bit into his sandwich.

"If I need a cold drink," Finn said with a wink, "I'll make it a Guinness." Max nodded and smiled at him with his mouth full.

"The library is done except for the fake book panels," I said looking at Evelyn who seemed to just pick at her food. "Maybe we could go into town and see how the artist is doing with them?" I thought maybe if I got her mind on something other than our first guest arriving this afternoon, she might relax a bit.

Evelyn gave me a half smile. "I don't want to leave the lodge in case our guest arrives earlier than planned." She picked up a slice of green pepper and took a small bite. "And I want to be sure everything is in order for our other guests who plan to arrive tomorrow."

"I thought we only had one for the weekend," Charles said.

"I got a phone call just before lunch." Rather than being excited about more guests, Evelyn looked uncomfortable. I was puzzled. "It seems that the parents of the boy who died want to come and stay here while they make the arrangements to repatriate his body. They said there is a lot of paperwork and. . ." Evelyn took a sip of her tea. ". . .and they want to visit the spot where their son died."

It got quiet around the table. We sat and studied our food for a few minutes. Evelyn took a deep breath and stood taking up her plate with a half-eaten sandwich still on it. She looked at all of us with tearful eyes. "I really wanted this to be a more cheerful beginning but I guess we'll take what we have and make the best of it. We'll have to make sure we still make it a nice visit for our other guest." She turned and took her plate to the sink.

Charles got up, walked to her and pulled her into his arms. "Ev, you are a gracious hostess and I'm sure that all of our guests will feel your care for them whatever their needs may be. We'll do our best to help comfort the parents and still entertain our other guest. We're all in this together, right?"

She lifted her head from his shoulder and smiled at him. He wiped tears from her eyes. The rest of us tried not to make it so obvious that we were so touched by their devotion to one another. My heart felt full. Charles was the most perfect match for my daughter I could ever have imagined or wished for. Surely God could see my grateful heart as I silently thanked him.

I helped Evelyn clean up from lunch. Millie went on home since we were done with preparing for guests and the library was cleaned and put in order. The men went out to the castle to work on positioning the trail camera. "What can I do for you now?" I asked Evelyn. "Cut vegetables? Brown the meat? Just get out of your way?"

Evelyn laughed. "How about you cut—" She didn't get to finish. Chaos came calling. The doorbell rang just as we heard a crash from the alcove by the kitchen door where the trashcan was. Allie came racing past us with her treasure in a small plastic bag. Evelyn's face paled. I could see the panic rise.

I grabbed her shoulders. "You get the door. I'll get the dog. We've got this!" I grabbed a roll of paper towels and a cloth and took off after Allie who left little traces of her treasure like a bread crumb trail. Thankfully it all cleaned up with a little wipe but in stopping to clean the trail as I went, I lost track of where she'd gone. I turned a couple of circles in the gathering room and spied another piece of toast at the door to the library. Closing the door behind me as I entered, I called out sweetly to Allie. "Here girl. Where are you, you sweet little package of trouble." I figured she couldn't understand the words, just the tone of my voice.

A tail thumped behind one of the chairs and I slowly approached it. At least with the door closed, she would be contained to one room. Behind the chair she was belly down and resting her head on what was left of the plastic bag. "What have you got?" I kept my voice soft and sing-songy as if talking to a child, which in a sense I was. Careful not to move too fast, I approached slowly, afraid she would grab it and run again and spread what was left all over my nice clean library. I guess she was done with it and the stir she'd caused. She stood up and let me pick up the pieces of leftover breakfast and whatever else was in there. I hadn't thought to grab an empty bag but I wrapped everything up in the cloth I had and wiped up the rug where some jam had stuck.

Just as I straightened up again, the door to the library opened and Allie sprinted for the door. She stopped just short of it as Evelyn and a rather tall man entered. Allie backed up a bit and sat with her tail wagging looking for some recognition from Evelyn. The man, who was dressed in a tweed suit with suede elbow patches, held a matching short brimmed walking hat in his hand. He switched the hat from one hand to the other and bent down to pet Allie. Allie stood, her ears laid back and her body tense. I could hear a low growl from her, something that we didn't hear very often from an otherwise cheerful and playful pup.

"Allie!" Evelyn put a hand on her collar and made her sit again. "I'm sorry," she said to the gentleman. "She's still a pup and we haven't had many visitors yet so she's not used to strangers."

"Not a problem." The man straightened quickly and looked around the room. His eyes came to rest on me. "And who is this lass?" He took a few steps forward.

"My mother," Evelyn said. "She's going to help us with keeping this beautiful place shipshape. Mom, this is Professor Thornbury, our guest for the next few days."

I walked toward them and then realized I couldn't very well hold out a hand to shake. "It's nice to meet you." I motioned with the paper towels and the bundle of garbage in the cloth. "Sorry my hands are kind of full right now. Our pup has been up to some mischief." I glared down at Allie who hung her head and let her ears droop to look dutifully penitent.

"Not a problem," he said. He took a few steps and turned with a slight frown. "You've made some changes in here."

"I'm sorry," said Evelyn sounding confused, "I didn't know you'd been here before."

"Ah, yes. Well," his speech seemed to falter. "I was. . .There was a friend of mine who knew the previous owner and I visited once with him." He turned back to the room and began to explore, squinting at times to read a book title. "There doesn't seem to be as many books as once were here. I hope they haven't been destroyed. I so admired the collection."

"No," I said. His visit must have been a lengthy one to know that the collection of books had been reduced. "We took many of the books that were older and donated them to the local library for their archives. The top shelves have been emptied so that our guests won't be climbing too high on the ladder to reach the reading material."

"Donated?" He gave a look of surprise. When he turned and looked up at the top shelves, he nodded. "Ah, yes. I see."

The man continued to examine the shelves of books. I looked at Evelyn and she shrugged slightly. I motioned with my head to the trash in my hands. "I need to get rid of this stuff." I tucked the roll of paper towels under my arm and switched the towel full of garbage to that hand as I reached down for Allie's collar. I wasn't sure I could count on her following me on her own. She was still studying our guest. "I'll get her out to the kitchen," I said to Evelyn. "Let me know if you need me."

Thankfully Allie didn't give me any trouble and I was able to get her to her dog crate where I ordered her to stay for a bit. She surprisingly obeyed and settled in with her head resting on her front paws. "If you behave, I'll take you for a walk later." Her head popped up at the walk word. "Not now." I held my hand out flat and motioned as I said, "Down, girl." She gave in with a sigh.

As I disposed of Allie's mess I thought back to her reaction to Professor Thornbury. I'd never seen Allie behave like that before. She tended to be too friendly to visitors. When all of the local police were here, she kept approaching them for a pat on the head. She'd never once growled at a delivery person. And she'd even managed to worm her way into Max's heart. I smiled. There was a gentle side to Max that I really appreciated. Hopefully with things mostly in order now, there would be a little more time to spend together. We still had this relationship thing to work out. I found myself humming as I started slicing vegetables for Evelyn's stew.

8

Evelyn came into the kitchen and gave a big sigh. Her hands covered her face for a moment as if she were trying to wipe away a thought. “What’s wrong, honey,” I asked. She looked exasperated.

“Apparently our guest is a vegetarian which he didn’t mention in his reservation information. He won’t be dining with us this evening.” She put her hands on her hips and looked around at the vegetables I’d already cut. “I guess it’ll just be us to have the Irish stew for dinner.”

I wiped my hands on a towel and gave her a hug. “It’s okay. Less pressure. You don’t have to worry about whether or not he likes the stew. He strikes me as being the kind of person who is a bit particular anyway.” I turned to finish cutting my last carrot. “So how does that change our breakfast menu?”

“He’s fine with toast and fruit and porridge,” she said as she started browning the lamb for the stew.

“Porridge?”

“Oatmeal works for that.” She took a shuddered breath.

Evelyn’s shoulders hunched. She was trying hard to control tears. A nursery rhyme came to mind.

“Pease porridge hot. Pease porridge cold. Pease porridge in the pot. Nine days old.” I chuckled. “Do we have any nine day old porridge we can offer him?”

Evelyn laughed and took a swipe at her eyes with the back of her hand. She turned to look at me with eyes that brimmed with tears. “I just wanted us to start out with a good experience and feel that we were successful in all that we planned and prepared for. Now, with a picky professor and a grieving family due to arrive it all seems overwhelming."

My heart hurt for her. "Evelyn, I haven't asserted myself as your mother in a while but I'm telling you right now—go blow your nose, dry your eyes and take a deep breath. You've got this. You faced plenty of challenges on that ship as cruise director with last minute changes and obstacles in your path. You can do this."

She nodded her head as she reached for the box of tissues on the counter in the corner. After she blew her nose and dried her eyes, she smiled at me. "Of course. You're right. I just don't know what's wrong with me lately. I seem to fall apart too easily." She took a deep breath. "Thanks, Mom. I needed that. I'll straighten up and fly right like Dad used to say."

While there wasn't a day when I didn't think of Paul, Max had made me miss him a little less, Evelyn's comment made my heart sink a bit. Paul was off enjoying Heaven while the rest of us were still muddling through life. I did wish that he could have seen what a beautiful woman his daughter had become. He'd be so proud.

Millie returned to help us with the afternoon tea. I was enjoying those moments when we all came together and had an afternoon break. Today would be a bit different as our guest, vegetarian or not, was taking tea as well. We finished setting out the hot water and a variety of teas that Evelyn had arranged in a box with sections in it so that the teas wouldn't mix together and one tea flavor the other. Millie had brought a variety of scones and pastries and some little sandwiches from the local bakery. Since it was Friday and a dinner night, we'd decided not to try to bake and take the time to make sandwiches as well. At least not for this first day of having a guest.

Professor Thornbury came in the front door from his walk and I met him in the entry to let him know that afternoon tea was ready and set in the dining room. He removed his hat and hung it on the coat tree then delicately balanced his walking stick in the corner behind it. "Thank you," he said. "I believe I saw a water closet off the hallway. I'll need to wash my hands."

"Of course," I said. I watched him walk down the hall. There was something about him that was a bit unnerving. Maybe it was his overly proper manner. I hadn't met any other Irish folk who seemed so uptight. Then maybe it was just that he was a professor. Perhaps he felt he deserved a little more respect for that.

Millie went into the dining room to be sure the professor had everything he needed. She came back out to the kitchen and said he would like us to join him since he was the only guest. The men who had come in from their work at the castle looked at each other and shook their heads.

"I don't think we're properly cleaned up to have tea in the dining room," Charles said. "Why don't you ladies join him?"

Millie and Evelyn looked at me and I shrugged. "I guess." The three of us took our teacups into the dining room and tried not to look nervous. We each took a plate and a few things to nibble on before we sat down.

"Ah, I thank you for joining me," Professor Thornbury said flashing a smile that showed rather large teeth. It reminded me a bit of a skeleton's smile. "I thought there might be a few more guests to join me in tea." He raised an eyebrow obviously indicating he expected some sort of reply to his comment.

"You are our first guest," Evelyn said with a nervous chuckle. "We just opened the Shamrock Bed and Breakfast but we are expecting more guests tomorrow."

"I see." Thornbury took a sip of his tea.

I thought it best to get some kind of conversation going that didn't focus on our nerves that were jangled on our first day of opening the lodge to guests. "If you don't mind my asking," I ventured, "what is it you teach Professor Thornbury?"

"Don't mind at all, young lady." The tone of his response sounded patronizing. "I teach the history of our glorious Ireland and some of the rich folk lore that has evolved over the centuries."

"That sounds very interesting," I said. "Where do you teach?"

"At the University College Dublin. Magnificent institution!" He waved his teacup in the air. The rest of us looked wide-eyed at each other over the rims of our teacups. We didn't say a word but we all remembered the poor boy who died was from that college. Could Thornbury have known him? Should we ask?

Evelyn stood. "I'm sorry. I have to excuse myself. The lamb stew is not going to make itself and I need to get it started." She looked a bit pale and I could imagine her thoughts ran to the parents of the boy who were due to arrive the next day. It could be awkward. "Mom, Millie, stay and enjoy the rest of your tea."

"Yes, please," said Thornbury, "please don't abandon me yet." He sort of smiled again. I felt like his face didn't really know what to do with a smile.

Now I hated when Max called me a sleuth, it sounded too much like a snoop, but label me curious as I asked the next question of Professor Thornbury. "Professor, you mentioned that you were here before and enjoyed the library. Were there some books of interest to you?"

Thornbury leaned against the back of his chair. He seemed to be mulling over my question. I thought it was pretty straight forward. Why was he being so careful in how he answered?

"I am a researcher as well as a teacher, Ms.. . . I'm sorry. Your name has escaped me."

"Stengel. Casey Stengel," I said smiling. "Evelyn only introduced me as her mom."

"Of course. Good that it's not my memory failing me." He reached for his pot of tea and poured the rest of it into his cup. "As I was saying, I am a researcher and my friend who directed me here thought I might find some interest in the older editions in the library that pertained to the history and folk lore that I study." He sipped his tea gingerly as if it were too hot which it couldn't possibly be at this point. Again, I had the feeling he was searching for the right thing to say. He put the cup down and leaned forward. "Might I ask what happened to so many of the older editions that were a part of the collection?"

Millie cleared her throat. "Our library in town was the recipient of those beauties. They are categorizing them and organizing them for their own collection. We have quite a good community library and much of it is devoted to the history of the area." The last was said with a note of pride in her voice. "Did you have time on your previous visit to explore our town library?"

"No. No, I wasn't here that long. I shall have to make sure to do that on this visit especially now that you tell me how valuable their collection must be."

Professor Thornbury drained the rest of the tea in his cup and stood. "Ladies, if you'll excuse me, I think I'll find my way into town and look for the library as well as a place to suit my dietary needs."

We stood as well and began clearing the table pausing only to see him through the window as he walked to his car. Millie shook her head. "That man bothers me." She bit her lower lip and shook her head again. "I git the feelin' he's acting the maggot."

I stopped stacking plates and cups on the tray and frowned at her. "What do you mean?" I asked.

"I've heard a lot of Irish brogues and accents but his is like some poor actor tryin' to be Irish. I'm not so sure he's even British." She shook her head again. "Just sumthin' about that man. He's acting the maggot." She looked at my puzzled expression and laughed. "That means he's up to no good."

Call it women's intuition or whatever else you may, Millie and I were both feeling uneasy about our first bed and breakfast guest.

9

The aroma of lamb stew, rich with onions, potatoes, carrots and of course Guinness to flavor it all filled the kitchen as we all assembled for dinner. Evelyn had set places for Millie and Finn who agreed to stay and eat with us. Millie said she had to sample the stew that Finn had crowed about. With a nod of her head and her eyes closed, she took a deep breath to inhale the aroma of the stew. "If it tastes half as good as it smells, I can see why Finn was so taken with it." She blew on her spoon and sampled a tender piece of lamb. "Mmmm. Perfect." She pointed her empty spoon at Evelyn. "Are you sure you're not Irish?"

Evelyn laughed. "Well there is the O'Shaugnessy side of mom's family so I guess there might be a bit of the Irish blood in my veins."

"Either that or she's just a really good cook," Charles said as he shoveled another large spoonful of stew into his mouth.

"I'll agree with the good cook assessment," I said. "Evelyn, is there anything you can't do?"

Instead of looking pleased, Evelyn's smile faded and she picked at a biscuit on her plate. "I can't prevent the pain I'm almost sure will be there tomorrow when that mother and father come to see where their son died." She looked up at me. "And when they discover that Professor Thornbury teaches at the same college their son attended, it's just possible it will add to their grief."

"Maybe not," I said as I searched for another sweet carrot in my bowl. Why did the carrots seem so much sweeter in Ireland? "Perhaps Professor Thornbury knew the boy and he can tell the parents something good about his studies."

"Professor Thornbury?" Millie huffed. "He dunna seem like a compassionate man." She shook her head as she had before at afternoon tea. "Sumthin' about that man."

I could almost see Max's ears perk. He'd finished his bowl of stew and was working on his third biscuit, the bread kind, not the cookie kind. "What do you mean, Millie?"

"His speech is strange. I can't place his accent. I've been many places in Ireland but never heard an Irishman speak as he does."

"Aye," said Finn. "I noticed too. He's a strange fellow."

"Very strange," Charles said reaching for another soft biscuit to dip in his stew gravy. "I don't understand his interest in the security cameras and the trail camera we're setting up at the castle. He was so insistent on knowing when it was installed, how it worked and what it could show. I'd like to think it was just a passing interest in what we were doing but I just have this weird feeling about him."

"He was pretty curious about the boy, too," Max said. He leaned back and patted his stomach. I smiled at the gesture of satisfaction in his meal. He might not always say nice things but his body language spoke volumes sometimes. "I don't get how he knew about the boy. Was it on the news or something?"

"It might have been in the Dublin papers, or the college paper if they have one," I said. "He teaches at the University College Dublin where the boy went to school. Maybe the news somehow got there that way."

"We keep saying 'the boy'," Evelyn said. "Don't we know his name? I know his parents' names are Patrick and Linda Kelly but they never said his name, just 'our son'."

"His name is James," Max said, "James Kelly. I'm sorry. I thought I told you all that." He shrugged apologetically and dove back into his stew while the rest of us paused.

"James," Millie said quietly. "Poor James."

A moment later the quiet was shattered by the sound of the front door slamming. Allie raised up from the floor on her haunches, a low growl deep in her throat. "Allie!" Charles said quickly as he put a hand on her back. "Sit. That's just our guest."

"I should go see if he needs anything," Evelyn said.

"No." I rose before she could move. "I'll check on him. You sit and enjoy the rest of this wonderful stew."

"Thanks, Mom," she said without argument but with a look of worry on her face.

"It'll be okay," I said as I turned and walked toward the hall to the foyer.

Professor Thornbury was hanging his coat on the coat tree stand near the entrance. Apparently the evening air had a chill that required an overcoat. Or was it all a part of his persona? His face was flushed and I wondered if he'd been drinking. It couldn't possibly be that cold outside. The look he gave me told me it wasn't cold or drinking. It was anger. What could he be so upset about?

"Good evening, Professor," I said quietly. "I hope you found what you needed in town. It's quite a lovely little place."

"Hmph," he said as he shrugged his tweed jacket back into place on his shoulders. "Your library closed quite early and I was forced to leave before I could finish my research." He picked at his sleeve as if removing a piece of lint. "Hopefully I will be treated with a bit more respect when I return tomorrow."

I took a deep breath and ventured forth with the

question I was supposed to ask, hoping that the answer would be reasonable. “Is there anything I can get for you?”

“No,” he said rather harshly and then seemed to soften. “I’m sorry. I don’t require anything else tonight but thank you.”

With that he trudged up the stairs to his room. I let out the breath I was holding. I was glad Evelyn had let me handle this. She didn’t need his attitude. Not tonight. Not with the anticipation of receiving poor James’ parents tomorrow. I hoped Thornbury’s attitude would not intrude on their grief.

10

While Millie helped Evelyn with the breakfast for Professor Thornbury, I went up to his room and let myself in to freshen the bathroom and make the bed. The room had a view of the castle and one of the lovely gardens that Finn took such care with. I paused a moment by the small mahogany writing desk that sat in front of the window to look out at the castle caught in the rays of the sun that promised to bring a cheery warm day.

When I turned to leave, I accidently bumped the desk and knocked a sheaf of papers to the floor. I scurried to pick them up and try to keep them in the order that they'd fallen so as not to let the Professor know I'd been so clumsy. Heaven forbid he should think I was snooping. As I set them back again where I thought they should be, the top page caught my eye. It looked like the title page to a manuscript. Was he writing a book?

In bold letters across the page was written "The Irish Crown Jewels, Fact Or Fiction?" Down further on the page was the author's name. Roger Callahan. Not Professor Thornbury? Was it someone else's manuscript? And why would the professor have it? Crown jewels? Irish crown jewels? My head was swimming.

I left quickly before he could return and find me staring at the pages. Much as I would have liked to read further, I didn't dare chance being discovered. It was enough that I may not have put it all back quite in the same order. My hands were shaking when I locked the door behind me.

As it was, Professor Thornbury never went back to his room after breakfast. When I came into the kitchen after making sure all was ready for the Kellys, Millie and Evelyn said that the professor had left immediately for the library to be there when it opened. Evelyn took her empty cup to the sink and turned with a sigh. "I'll be in the office if you need me."

"Thornbury was pretty upset last evening about having to leave the library before he was finished with his research," I said as I sat down to join Millie for a morning coffee break. "So angry his face was flushed."

"I donna doubt it," said Millie. She reached for a mini blueberry muffin. "Sarah said he was awful to her as she had to shoosh him out of the door when they closed."

"So much for pretending to be a gentleman, I guess." I popped one of Evelyn's little muffin gems into my mouth.

"It was very strange," Millie went on. "Sarah called me to tell me about it. She was upset that he wanted to go through all the books that we donated from the library. He claimed there was important research in those books that he needed to find for his work."

I raised my coffee cup to my lips and paused. The manuscript I'd seen in his room came to mind. Was that his work? And if it was, why was the author's name Roger Callahan? Was he using a pen name? Having noted his rather big ego, I couldn't imagine him not taking credit for his own work. I took a sip of coffee. Maybe when I had a little more time I could do an internet search on the name. I swallowed the last bit of my coffee and rose.

"Guess it's time to see what Evelyn might need help with," I said to Millie who was already rinsing our cups for the dishwasher. "I think the rooms are all ready."

"I'll open the windows a bit in the Kellys' room," Millie said wiping her hands with a nearby towel. "Always smells better when the fresh air comes in."

I found Evelyn in her office at the computer frowning at the screen. I gently put a hand on her shoulder.

"What's up? You look a bit worried."

She reached up and patted my hand then leaned back in her chair. "The company wants us to post No Trespassing signs by the castle. They are concerned that if anyone else gets hurt there they might be held liable."

"Surely not," I said placing my hands on either side of the base of her neck and massaging. "Who in their right mind would want to dig around a collapsing castle and not take responsibility for what might happen?"

"Mmmm, that feels so good," said Evelyn closing her eyes and yielding to the relaxing motion of my hands. "I don't know Mom. Maybe they are overreacting. I've never seen No Trespassing signs anywhere around here. If we put them up, I wonder what the locals will think?"

"How many locals really come up and explore the castle?" I asked sitting in the chair next to her desk. "If we position the signs near the collapsed wall, most probably won't even see them and you'll still be following instructions."

Evelyn put fingers to her temples and massaged them. "You're right. I'm just not thinking straight. I have to stop worrying so much. I don't know what's going on with me."

"Are you feeling okay?" I reached out and put a hand to her forehead as I'd done so often when she was a child. It was cool. "You don't have a fever. Are you getting enough sleep?" I sat down in the chair across from her.

"I am but I'm still tired all the time." She sighed and shook her head. "Maybe everything is finally catching up with me. We went full speed ahead getting all of this ready."

"You need a little time off. Let's plan to give you some in the next day or two once we've gotten our new guests settled. Millie and I can handle breakfast and tea and do the rooms. You don't need to worry about dinner again for a while." I sat in the chair next to her and patted her knee. "I'll bet that husband of yours would love to take you somewhere nice to enjoy a day together."

Evelyn smiled at me. "You always seem to know what I need. I love you."

"I love you too, honey. Now," I said as I slapped my knees and rose from the chair, "let's get the rest of our morning chores done before those hungry men come in for lunch." Charles and Max were outside staining and sealing some of the wood trim that had been neglected for so many years.

Evelyn turned back to her computer. "I still have a few responses to give to some inquiries about the Shamrock. It looks like we may have some more guests in another week or so."

"Wonderful! I imagine we will really begin to rock and roll before long." I made some gestures with my hands as if I were rocking to music.

Evelyn laughed. "I think it's more hip hop today."

"Like a bunny hop?"

Evelyn just smiled and shook her head. "I think you better stick to your baseball analogies. You have a better chance of hitting a homerun."

Now I had to laugh. "Look at you! A grand slam!"

In the back closet next to the laundry, I picked up my basket of cleaning supplies and grabbed a couple of cleaning rags from the shelf. When I went to tuck them into the basket, I noticed a rag there that I hadn't taken out to put in the wash bag. I reached in and pulled it out. As I did, it unrolled and released the package of letters I had wrapped in it. In all the flurry of activity, I'd forgotten about them. I set the basket back on the shelf and took the letters to my room. I didn't have time to peruse them just now but I would later and if I set them on the nightstand, I would remember.

I retrieved my cleaning basket again and started through the gathering room making sure I dusted all the table tops and nooks and crannies. I'd learned in my years of household managing that dust webs didn't take any time to form and you had to keep after them. I didn't find any but I ran the duster over everything anyway. In a few days, I would add a bit of polish as well.

The library still needed finishing. The fake book fronts that would fill the upper shelves had been delivered by the artist in town and Max had promised to secure them as soon as he could. Several books were strewn haphazardly on the coffee table. I wondered if Thornbury had been in here again going through the shelves of books. What was he looking for? A thought struck me. Could it be the letters? Maybe it had nothing to do with books and everything to do with the letters.

I made a promise to myself to look over those letters just as soon as our baseball date was over tonight. Charles had recorded another Dodgers' game for Max and me to watch. It wasn't as satisfying as keeping up with them in real time but real time was a whole lot different here than there and it wasn't just the time zone changes. We were really busy keeping everything on track at the lodge. I wondered if once we got into a rhythm or more of a regular schedule, things would get a little less hectic. Then again, we did have some unusual goings on to deal with before we'd even made it to first base but I was sure we'd be hitting home runs before long.

I'd finished dusting and straightening the library and was headed back through the gathering room to return my cleaning basket when I heard Evelyn greeting the Kellys who had just arrived.

"Of course I am sorry for the circumstances that have brought you here," Evelyn said, "but I hope you will be comfortable and please, if there is anything we can do to help you through this, let us know." Evelyn saw me as I stood in the doorway. "Oh, this is my mother who is here helping us out. Mom," she said as politely as I'd taught her, "this is Mr. and Mrs. Kelly."

I nodded. My hands were full of cleaning supplies so I couldn't offer one to shake. "I'm sorry we have to meet in such a difficult time for you. As Evelyn said, please let us know if we can do anything for you. I believe Millie has your room all refreshed and ready for you."

"Thank you," said Mrs. Kelly who looked tired and worn probably from the travel as much as the grief they experienced. "Please call us Patrick and Linda." She tried a smile but it kind of quivered and disappeared.

I nodded. "And please call me Casey. I only answer to Mom when Evelyn calls." That got a little wider smile from Linda but Patrick remained sullen.

"Let me show you to your room," said Evelyn as she waved a hand toward the stairway, "I'm sure you're ready to refresh and maybe rest a bit."

As they followed Evelyn up the stairs, Patrick said, "We'd like to see where James was when he died."

"Of course," said Evelyn. "Please don't go over to the castle though without someone from the lodge. It's very dangerous. The walls have been weakened by the digging that was done. I'll get my husband or Finn to take you over there when you're ready."

"Digging?" Patrick paused a moment. "What sort of digging? Are they excavating the castle?"

Evelyn continued up the stairs not turning to look at Patrick as she answered. "No excavation. The digging has been a mystery to us. We're not sure but we think James may have been doing some when the wall collapsed on him."

I held my breath. What would be the Kellys' response to know that their son might have caused his own death by digging at the base of the castle wall? They continued on to their room without another comment. I turned and headed down the hallway to put away my cleaning supplies. What was James doing at the castle? Digging? What did he hope to find?

After lunch I found Max in the library installing the last of the fake book fronts on the top two shelves of the book cases. "Are you all finished with your outdoor work?" I asked.

"Are you checking up on me?" he said giving me his eyebrows raised Clooney look.

"No," I said feeling a little heat rise to my face. "I didn't mean to make it sound that way. I was just curious and grateful that you have the time to finish this project for us."

Max backed down the ladder with a screwdriver in his mouth. I was going to say something about that being dangerous but I held my tongue. No need to evoke the Bogart side of him. When he reached the bottom of the ladder he stepped back and looked up at his work.

"That artist did a great job," he said putting his hands on his hips as he nodded his head slightly with approval. He turned to me. "In answer to your question, Charles is taking the Kellys over to the castle and we decided to just hang it up for today. I have the afternoon free. How about you?"

"My work is done except for afternoon tea. What are you thinking?"

"I was thinking about going into town and looking around. Maybe looking for that friendly dolphin that's supposed to be around there. Maybe even looking for a pub for a Guinness and chips with a special lady." There was a twinkle in his eye.

"And who would that special lady be?" I asked, my hands on my hips.

"Why the one standing before me, of course." With that, Max planted a sweet kiss on my cheek. "I just need to shower and change clothes. Let me know when you're ready."

"Won't be long," I said following him out of the library. "Maybe Millie won't need me for tea."

An hour later, Max and I were in the extra car that Charles and Evelyn had leased and headed into town. I was a little nervous riding with Max since he hadn't had all that much experience driving on the left side of the road. He seemed just fine and I relaxed a bit. It was good to get out of the lodge for a spell and see the countryside again. I made a note to myself that we needed to set time aside to do that regularly just as I'd suggested to Evelyn. We all needed a break now and then from routine and certainly our routine had been rather difficult to start with.

The harbor was as breathtaking as my first look at it had been when Finn drove me to the lodge from the airport. There was not much wind today so the waters were calm with small ripples. We drove slowly through town. Colorful buildings of blue, green, red, yellow and even pink enchanted me. Some were painted with emblems on their facade and a couple with shamrocks. The roads were narrow and it made me more than a little nervous as we navigated through unfamiliar places with directional markers that were a little confusing to someone who was used to driving on the other side of the road. I didn't want Max to think I was criticizing his driving but I thought if we got out and walked, I would enjoy it more.

"Max, do you think you could find a place to park?" I said as sweetly as I could. "I would love to get out and walk and look in some of the pubs and stores."

"Good idea," Max said. "No need to waste a perfectly good day with sunshine and fresh sea air in a car."

I relaxed. I wondered if he was feeling a little tense driving in unfamiliar territory. We found a small parking lot near the main docks that offered tours of the harbor. Before we got out of the car, Max pointed to a sign that indicated one hour tours of the harbor and the chance to see the famous dolphin, Fungie. "Are you up for a boat ride?" he asked.

"Are we dressed warm enough?" I asked. "It could be colder out there on the water." I fumbled in my pockets and found some gloves that I'd stuffed in there when I had taken Allie for a walk around the lodge grounds. I pulled them out and held them up. "I can keep my hands warm at least."

Max smiled. "Well," he said as he pulled out a pair of work gloves from his pockets, "seems I can too."

He twisted to look in the back seat. "And it looks like there's a blanket in the back seat for some reason. Were Charles and Evelyn planning on a picnic somewhere?" Now he was grinning. Had he planned all this?

"Guess it's settled." I chuckled. "Let's go!"

We managed to be there at just the right time. There was room on the very next boat heading out and it didn't take long to be settled into a seat and on our way. The sun was shining but the wind kicked up as the boat moved out and gave me a bit of a chill. Max and I wrapped the blanket around us and snuggled a bit together. There was quite a lot of history in the commentary from our tour guide and captain. Birds soared high above the red sandstone cliffs we passed. Suddenly we saw a group of birds dive into the water. The tour guide explained that they were gannets diving for mackerel. To add to my Irish folklore, the guide also told of the plot hatched by Count James Louis Rice to help Marie Antoinette escape to Ireland. The plan never worked because she wouldn't leave without the king. "You might say she lost her head over him" was part of the tour guide's humor for the day.

I looked at Max who seemed to be more absorbed in the water and the feeling of being on the sea again. I gave him a little poke. "Are you missing your boat?"

He turned to me with a slight frown and then smiled. "Yeah, maybe a little. I miss the feeling of freedom it gave me, the thrill of skimming atop the waves and the tug of a fish on the line knowing that dinner would be good that night." He shrugged. "But I'm enjoying new adventures with you." He hugged me a bit closer. It felt good to be in his embrace.

Our moment of closeness was interrupted abruptly by shouts of "Over there!" We looked in the direction people were pointing and suddenly saw a dolphin pop up into the air, do a perfect pirouette and disappear into the water only to reappear a little closer to us and perform again. Fungie, the famous dolphin of the harbor followed us quite awhile as we slowly made our way back to the docks. He had been performing for tourists since he got separated from his dolphin friends some years ago.

The boat tied up to the dock and we all thanked our guide for a great time. We were feeling quite pleased with our afternoon so far. Max tossed the blanket back in the car and we took off on a walk through town. At the first pub we found, we ducked inside. The wind was beginning to kick up a bit and we were still a little chilled from our boat tour. Max still wanted a Guinness but I opted for warm tea. While we waited for our order to arrive, I noticed a familiar figure tucked in a booth in the corner.

I leaned closer to Max and nodded in the direction of the booth. “Isn’t that Thornbury?” I half whispered, not that Thornbury could have heard me from where we were sitting with all the noise in the pub. Max nodded and gave that Columbo look as he studied Thornbury. The man had a cell phone to his ear and was gesturing as if he were arguing with the person on the other end of the call. Curious. Or as Alice would say, curiouser and curiouser.

The manuscript I’d seen came to mind again and the name Peter Callahan. Should I tell Max? I knew he would start calling me a sleuth again but I figured I could handle his teasing. What could it hurt? He was so good at figuring out things especially when they might be linked to a crime. Did I seriously think there was a crime associated with Thornbury? He certainly seemed suspicious enough. My tea arrived with Max’s Guinness. I looked at him still studying Thornbury and decided we needed to work together on this. After all, we did make a good team.

Team! I’d almost forgotten. We had a ballgame to watch tonight. Maybe I’d tell him then.

11

As it happened, I decided not to wait until the baseball game to tell Max. I didn't want the subject of Thornbury intruding on our date. On the way back to the lodge, Max suddenly pulled the car to the side of the road and turned it off. "How about hot dogs for our game tonight?" He sounded like a kid at Christmas.

"Hot dogs?" I looked at him with surprise. "Where are we going to get hot dogs?"

Max pointed to a blue trailer parked along the street called the Dingle Doghouse. "Right there. The sign says American hot dogs. Should we give it a try? We can have him wrap them up and we can reheat them for the game at home."

I laughed. "Sounds like a plan. I wonder if they really taste like home though?"

"Well, can't hurt to try." Max had me wait in the car while he rounded up the hot dogs and came back with two cans of Coke as well. "Now that's really a little bit of home away from home." He put the Cokes and dogs in the back seat and turned to start the car. "Do you know what Bogart always said?" I looked at him warily and shook my head. "A hot dog at the game beats roast beef at the Ritz." He grinned.

So that was it. He had a Bogart persona for sure. Well, I hated to put that aside but I did need to tell him about Thornbury. I clasped his arm as he reached to turn the car back on. "I have to tell you something." Max looked at me for a moment but didn't say anything. Instead, he relaxed and sat back as if he had all the time in the world to listen. He must have sensed my distress. I took a deep breath and confessed to my discovery of the manuscript and its author, Peter Callahan. It produced the anticipated result.

"So you were sleuthing again, huh?" he said in a teasing tone as he started the car and pulled out onto the road to head for the lodge. I could see his eyebrow raise. Bogart and Clooney step aside. Here comes Columbo.

"Not sleuthing," I protested. "I told you it was an accident."

"Sweetheart, I've told you before there are very few accidents and definitely no coincidences."

"This wasn't a coincidence. It was an accidental discovery."

"Ah, but an important one if what my gut is telling me about Thornbury is right. That man has something he's hiding. Millie's been suspicious of him from the beginning. And didn't you tell me Allie wasn't too fond of him either when they met? Dogs have a sixth sense about who they can or can't trust."

We made plans to look into Peter Callahan and Professor Thornbury online. With two of us searching, we were bound to find something. I did make Max promise that there would be no researching during the ballgame. I wanted to enjoy the game and the dogs and the Coke.

The Dodgers were having a bad year. Injuries and pitching woes were working against them this season. Still it was fun to watch the recorded game with my fellow Dodger fan and yell at the TV as things went badly. The hot dogs were almost like back home and the Cokes were great. I made some microwave popcorn in the fifth inning and finally when the Washington Nationals pulled ahead by ten in the eighth, we decided to call it a game and get down to some investigating. I refused to call it sleuthing.

Each of us sat with our laptops on our knees and began searching for Callahan and Thornbury. I scored first with a hit on Roger Callahan. A Roger Callahan had been a history professor and researcher at William and Mary

College in Williamsburg, Virginia. The article I found was congratulating him on his retirement and listed quite a few achievements and awards for his research. And here's where I got excited, it was on Irish history and folklore!

"Bingo!" I said, raising my hands in the air. "I've got Callahan!"

"Are you sure?" Max said calmly looking up from his screen.

Maybe my excitement was a bit much and it certainly wasn't a race to see who was going to score first but sleuthing or not, I was getting into this. "It's got to be. See here," I said pointing to my computer screen, "it says he was a professor of history specializing in Irish folklore. That manuscript was about the Irish crown jewels. He's written lots of other papers apparently on other topics dealing with Ireland's history."

"Okay," said Max slowly. He nodded his head absorbing what I had told him. "Bookmark that page so we can reference it later."

I created a new file labeled Shamrock Secrets and stored the bookmark there. I looked at Max bent over his screen frowning at whatever he was reading. "What do you have?"

"I have a list of faculty at the Dublin University where Thornbury is supposed to work but I don't see his name listed anywhere." Max sat back. "Did Evelyn get a home address for him? How did she know he was a professor there?"

"I don't know. I'd have to ask her. When she introduced him to me she referred to him being a professor but I don't know how she knew he was at least not until he told me where he worked."

"We need to follow up on that," said Max with a big sigh. I had the feeling his search was not turning out as well as mine had.

It was getting late and I couldn't hold back a big yawn. Max gave one in return. He looked at me and grinned. "Guess we've had ourselves quite a day. Maybe we need to give it a rest."

I nodded. "My eyes are getting blurry. I saved this site and can come back to it later." I closed my laptop. "Shall we meet again tomorrow and continue our search?"

"Sure," said Max rising slowly and stretching. I stood to see him to the door but he put down his laptop and pulled me into his arms. "I've enjoyed every minute of today with you. Thank you for letting me be a part of your life." With that he gently kissed me and said, "Good night, sweetheart."

Bogart, Clooney and Colombo all left and I stood there staring at the door that closed gently. I'd enjoyed today as well. I had enjoyed his company no matter what personality was showing. All the personas made one very interesting man and I felt my heart do a little something at the thought of his kiss.

I was tired but my curiosity was still nagging me after I got ready for bed. I snuggled under the covers and opened my laptop which still showed the article about Callahan. I read on through all the accolades and then came to the clincher. When asked what he was going to do after retirement, Callahan reported that he had purchased a castle in Ireland and was looking forward to spending his remaining days in peace enjoying his music and his books. A castle! Ireland! Could it be? Was Shamrock the castle? How would I find out? And how was I going to sleep tonight with that question spinning in my head like a curve ball headed for the plate.

I fell asleep with my laptop next to me and woke the next morning with the corner of it poking me as if it was nagging me to pick it up and pursue the questions I had from the night before. I didn't have time. I plugged it in to charge, made my bed and I scurried to get dressed and down to the kitchen to see if they needed help. By the time I did, Millie and Evelyn had everything under control and were just waiting on our guests to come for breakfast.

The coffee was hot. I grabbed a cup along with a nice cinnamon muffin for breakfast. As soon as the guests were in the dining room, I would go up and straighten their rooms. Charles was just finishing up his breakfast as I sat down.

"Morning," he said.

"Isn't is 'top o'the morning'?" I answered with a smile.

He nodded. "Sure and tis a great mornin' it is."

"You're getting more and more Irish every day." I winked at him and took a sip of coffee. "How did the Kellys do with the trip to the castle where James died?"

The smile faded from Charles' face. "It was pretty sad. Linda really broke up. I think she'd been holding it in for quite some time." He picked at some muffin crumbs on the table. "They just don't understand what he was doing there. Patrick said the last they had heard from him, he was doing a special research paper for his Irish folklore class. He'd been to some seminar off campus that had him all excited about the possibility of solving the mystery to some jewel theft."

"The Irish crown jewels? That would explain some things if he thought the jewels were actually buried at the castle."

"I guess." Charles rose. "There hasn't been any more digging since James died so it must have been him." He picked up his plate and cup. "I hope no one else from that seminar gets the same idea."

A seminar. I made a mental note to do some more online searching for what may have triggered James' interest in the castle. I also remembered that I had a couple of books in my room about castles and one in particular about the crown jewels. Could they hold some clues? My thoughts were interrupted by the voices of our guests coming from the dining room. I pushed my chair back and drained the last of my coffee from the cup. Time to get my work done. If I finished early enough maybe I could get some more time to go online and find some answers.

The morning chores went smoothly. The manuscript was gone from Thornbury's desk so I couldn't get a second look at it. I wondered if he noticed that it had been disturbed. The Kellys' room was neatly kept and all I needed to do was make the bed, wipe up the bathroom a bit and add fresh towels. The rest of the place was ship shape so I was done well before tea time. I checked on Evelyn who was back in the office working on her computer.

"How's it going, honey?" I asked.

Evelyn looked up and leaned back in her chair. "Well," she said pushing her hair back from her face. "It's going well. I think I'm finally getting the hang of this reservations software and we are getting some definite commitments for next month. We should be kept busy."

"All the more reason for you and Charles to slip off somewhere for a day and get some time together away from here before it gets too busy."

"Okay," she said with a smile. She rose from her chair and arched her back. "I need to move a little. We don't need to do tea this afternoon so I let Millie go home early. Care to take Allie for a walk with me?"

"No tea?" I asked. It seemed that Thornbury rather enjoyed his tea in the afternoon. I understood the Kellys not coming to tea. I had heard that they were meeting with authorities to work on repatriating James. Repatriating seemed like a strange term but I guess it was a little softer than just saying we are shipping his body home.

"The professor said he would be in town at tea time and would take it there," Evelyn said as we moved to the door of the office.

I paused. "Evelyn, how did you know he was a professor at University College Dublin?"

She shrugged. "He gave his address in Dublin and when I asked what he did there, he said he was a professor at the college specializing in Irish history and folklore."

"So it was just his word? Nothing on paper?"

She shrugged again and gave me a questioning look. "Yes. Why? He prepaid for his several nights stay and there was no reason to doubt that what he said was true. Is there something I should know?"

"Max and I are trying to figure him out. Max looked through the faculty listings online and couldn't find him. He thinks there might be something fishy there."

"Max does have a nose for that sort of thing." Evelyn rubbed her temples. "I hope there's nothing wrong that we have to deal with again. We've had enough for now." She put an arm around me. "How about that walk?"

Allie was so excited she could hardy contain herself and strained at the leash until she finally tired out a bit. She still looked at the flocks of birds that landed around the castle and flew off again periodically. The herding instinct in her showed through, there was no doubt about that. Blue skies dotted with a few puffs of clouds let the sun shine through enough to warm us a bit. A cool breeze though reminded us it was still spring in Ireland. It would be heating up back home in Florida about now. The humidity would be climbing. A little whiff of homesickness surprised me. There was nowhere else I'd rather be than here helping Evelyn and Charles and spending time with Max. Still, all the newness of a strange place was unsettling sometimes.

We had decided to walk around the outside of the castle, giving it plenty of respect in how close we came to its walls. As we passed the place where the wall had most recently crumbled, we saw the flowers that the Kellys had placed near where James died. A little wave of sadness came over us and we both sighed. We didn't need to exchange words to know what the other was feeling. As we passed the side of the castle that faced the lodge, we noticed an area of freshly turned soil. Evelyn stopped and put her hands on her hips.

"Not again," she said in a frustrated cry. Allie seemed to sense the moment and quieted. She sat and looked up at Evelyn. Maybe she thought she'd done something wrong. I patted her head which made her stand and start sniffing the ground.

"What would someone be doing digging around here now?" I started forward to look at the new dig with Evelyn right behind me. We stood at the edge of an almost square section of freshly turned soil. "Whoever did the digging certainly was rather neat about it."

We jumped when a voice behind us said, "Ah, that would be me and thanks for the good words. I tried me best to make it square." The distinct Irish sound of his voice told us it was Finn. We turned to find him holding a tray of green plants. "I've an idea for a new garden area. I was going to surprise you, Miss Casey, but you've found me out." His freckled cheeks puffed up as a broad grin spread across his face.

"Me? Why me?" I asked confused by his remark.

"Remember your first day in the car as we came back and you were sad that there were no shamrocks around a castle called Shamrock? Well, with a little bit o'luck we'll be havin' a field of shamrocks to grace the old walls of this place." He lifted the tray of plants to indicate that was what he was about.

"Oh Finn! What a delightful idea!" Evelyn said.

"I didn't mean to make more work for you, Finn," I said as I walked over to him and touched the leaves of the green shamrocks he held. "These are a little different than the ones back home."

"Aye." Finn nodded. "I'm sure you're not familiar with the hardy breed we need here to weather our climate and the rocks they need to grow 'round. Hopefully these will catch and prosper and live up to their reputation of bringing us good luck."

"Heaven knows we could use some," Evelyn said. "Well, Finn, we'll leave you to your work."

"Would you like a bit of help?" I asked him. "I don't think I'm needed at the house for a while. I'd love to get my hands a little dirty." I chuckled.

"Oh, I wouldn't be wantin' those lovely hands getting dirty," he set the tray down. "But I'd have an extra set of gloves in the truck if you'd like them."

"Deal!" I said suddenly feeling a sense of purpose that washed away the little nudge of homesickness I'd felt. I handed the leash for Allie to Evelyn. "Ev, do you mind?"

She laughed. "Of course not." She looked to Finn. "Keep her out of trouble, Finn. She has a bad habit of digging up dead bodies."

I put my hands on my hips. "Evelyn!" Finn was trying hard to contain his laughter. He finally understood the dead body references I got teased with.

12

Max reached out and brushed a thumb gently across my cheek. "You got a little sun today, didn't you, my little gardener."

"I see my status has changed from sleuth to gardener. I welcome the promotion." I laughed. "I really enjoyed working outside with Finn this afternoon. There's something about gardening that makes it peaceful and refreshing and since I've missed going to church, it was nice to enjoy a little peaceful reflection out there. I hope I did the planting correctly. I'd love to see those shamrocks prosper."

We finished setting the kitchen table for dinner. It was just the four of us tonight. Finn had left after our garden project was finished, excited about a special dinner Millie had promised him for tonight. Our dinner smelled really good. Evelyn asked Charles to lift it out of the oven for her. He set it on the stovetop and took a deep breath inhaling the wonderful aroma.

"If this tastes half as good as it smells, you have another winner to add to your trophy case of recipes." He put his arms around her and kissed the top of her head.

"Well," said Evelyn pulling back from his embrace, "it's not my recipe it's Millie's. She said it's the same one they use at the Fungie pub. She's friends with the cook there. Grew up with him. I hope I made it correctly."

"Well, let's test it out," I said as I pulled a couple of hot pads from the drawer to set on the table for the casserole dish. "All that gardening made me hungry."

Evelyn had Charles take the casserole to the table. She took a large spatula and cut square shapes into the casserole and began to place a serving on each of our plates as we passed them to her. Layers of ground lamb, peas and carrots, fluffy mashed potatoes and melted white cheddar cheese spread out on the plate and invited a taste. After Charles said grace, my first bite told me I was in love with this new recipe. I closed my eyes and gave a little moan. "Mmmmm. Perfect."

Max nodded his head as he scooped up another forkful of casserole. "Just as good as at the Fungie." Then he shook his head. "No, more so. Better." Max had been the one to order shepherd's pie at the pub when we all had dinner with Mille and Finn.

"It wasn't that hard to make either," said Evelyn balancing another bite on her fork. "I learned something else from Millie. It's not called shepherd's pie in Ireland. They just put that name on the menu because the tourists are more familiar with it. It's actually called cottage pie and the difference is that it's made with lamb instead of beef."

"The gravy is so flavorful," I said. "What's in it?"

Evelyn smiled and looked from Charles to Max. "The men are enjoying the flavor of Guinness in the broth."

I chuckled. "Well I'd rather have Guinness in the broth than Guinness in my glass." Guiness seemed to give me a stomach ache.

We finished our dinner off with coffee and some pastries that were leftover from the tea that didn't happen in the afternoon. When the guys sat back and patted their stomachs, I knew we were done and started clearing the rest of the dishes from the table. As I started to rinse the dishes and add them to the dishwasher, Max came up behind me and put his hands on my shoulders. "Do you mind if I come late to our sleuthing party?"

"Our what?!" I looked over my shoulder at him and frowned.

"You know. We planned to do a little online research together tonight but Charles asked if I'd help him get the disk from the trail camera to see what we might have on it and see if it's adjusted properly to get a clear view of the castle wall. He wants to get it done before it gets too dark."

"As long as you bring the coffee with you, you can come late." I smiled at him and put a wet finger on his nose.

"Hey!" he said backing away quickly. "See you in a little bit."

Evelyn came over to the sink with a couple of things to wash. "I think the boys were afraid we'd make them do dishes." She chuckled. A big yawn followed. "I think that fresh air this afternoon got to me."

"I can handle the rest of the dishes," I said. "There's not that many. You are a neat cook." Evelyn had a way of cleaning up as she cooked so there wasn't a lot to clean up once the meal was ready. "Did you ask Charles about a day off?"

"I did. Would Thursday work?"

"Sure," I said. "The Kellys will be gone by then and we have no new guests until the following week. If Thornbury stays any longer, I'd be surprised."

"I'll be glad when he's gone," said Evelyn. She handed me the empty casserole dish. "Looks like everyone enjoyed the cottage pie. I'll have to put it on the menu again. Maybe for one of our Friday dinners if any of our guests actually decide to dine with us."

"Honey, it will all work out and run like clockwork once we get in the swing of things." I took the casserole and rinsed the residue from it before putting it in the dishwasher. "We've had a rough start but it can only get better from here on out."

"I hope so." Evelyn yawned again.

"Go," I said waving my hands to shoo her out of the kitchen. "Get into something comfortable and curl up with a good book for the rest of the evening. I have a feeling we won't be seeing the guys for a while."

I was right. Charles and Max were gone for quite a while and I had time to slip into some loungewear and put my feet up on the sofa while I held my laptop on my knees and searched, or sleuthed as Max would say, for more information on Peter Callahan and Professor Thornbury. I discovered Callahan had never married and if he had a family, there wasn't any connection mentioned in what I'd found. Was he still alive? I plugged in the words "Peter Callahan obituary" and came up with a short paragraph about him dying in Ireland and being buried in the land he'd grown to love. It seemed strange that there was not more mention of him anywhere considering his long list of achievements I'd found on other sites.

More searching followed but my eyelids were getting heavy reading through all of Peter Callahan's achievements and accolades, I found once again the reference to him looking forward to spending retirement in Ireland. There had to be more somewhere. I yawned and stretched and looked at my watch. Where was Max? How long did he think I would wait up for him? A soft knock came on my door. I closed my laptop and uncurled my legs. "Coming," I called out.

When I opened the door, Max rushed in. His face was lit with excitement. "Oh good," he said, "you're still up."

"What is it?" I watched as he began pacing the floor. "Sit down and tell me." I pointed to the sofa.

"I'm not staying long," Max said continuing to pace but a bit slower now. "We took the memory card from the camera and plugged it into Charles' computer to have a look and see if we needed to adjust the camera to get a better view. We found some very interesting photos and video." He stopped pacing and when he looked at me I could see the old Max, the one who resembled Columbo when he was on a case and trying to solve it.

"Well, are you going to tell me what you found?" I smiled at him. I could see his mind racing a mile a minute.

"Oh, yes," he said, "of course." He ran a hand through his hair. "There were the pictures and video of the Kellys putting flowers where their son died and several of gulls landing and taking off. Then there were some nighttime photos that got very suspicious."

"Suspicious? How?"

"The camera wasn't positioned quite right to get a good view of who it was but someone was moving about near the collapsed wall." He paused as if drawing the suspense out. "The video was a little more telling than the still shots. The best we could tell, it looks like someone was using a metal detector and going over the area near where James died."

"A metal detector? How could you tell?"

"We could make out a sweeping motion of what looked like a stick. It took us a minute to figure out that must be what it was. Someone is still looking for something there at the castle." He finally sat down on the sofa.

"Was there more evidence of digging?" I sat at the other end of the sofa and hugged my knees to my chest.

"Nothing other than the area where you and Finn worked today."

I put my feet down on the floor and sat up straight. "It wasn't trampled was it?"

He smiled and patted my knee. "No, as far as we could tell your shamrocks are all intact. I think they are planted far enough from the castle walls that no one would bother them." He scratched his head. "Whatever these people think is there, is in the castle, not outside. I just hope we can catch them before there's more damage or life lost."

He rose and was halfway to the door when he suddenly turned and came back to sit down again and took my hand in his. "I'm sorry I missed our sleuthing party."

He grinned impishly knowing that the word sleuthing would rankle me. “Did you have any luck?”

I shook my head. “Not really. I stuck to searching through what I could find on Callahan and the only thing new is that he didn’t have any family that I could find and he died in Ireland but I couldn’t find out the circumstances or where he’s buried. It was just a short paragraph.”

“Strange,” said Max, “After all that recognition you found of him at retirement, you’d think more would have shown up.”

“I’m not done searching yet,” I said as I tried to stifle a yawn. “My eyes are beginning to swim though. I think I need to call it a night.”

“Me too,” said Max and he rose again. This time I walked him to the door and was rewarded with a soft kiss on my forehead as he left. It brought a warm feeling to me as I closed the door behind him. I could feel my heart growing fonder of him.

It was late and as much as I wanted to continue my investigation—there was no way I would label it sleuthing, I knew it was time to call it a night. I reached for a small notebook that I had always kept for notes about what needed to be done as I took care of a household. I was a good and conscientious household manager and was proud of my sense of organization. It was time to use that organization skill to keep a list of where I might look for answers and what I might be looking for.

When I was done making notes, I had a nice list of things to look into including the letters that I’d found and still hadn’t read. Then there was the possibility of Callahan owning Shamrock Castle and the lodge at some time. I was about to put the notebook away when I remembered one more thing. I opened it again and added a note to my list so I would remember to search for any seminars that James may have been interested in. Something sent him searching in the castle and digging up the wall. What was it?

13

Monday morning began with a cool misty fog that shrouded the castle walls and made it appear mysterious but a bit foreboding as well. I hoped there would be enough sunshine to melt it away. With all the nice sunny days we'd had, I guess I was spoiled. Well, one gray day was okay. I hoped that was all it would be.

Millie was already in the kitchen stirring the oatmeal I now called porridge that Thornbury insisted on each morning. "Can I help with anything?" I asked. I looked around and noticed that Evelyn was missing. "Where's Evelyn?"

Millie gave me a sly smile. "She's feelin' a bit uneasy this morning," she said. "I'm sure tis nothing to worry about."

"I don't know about that." I hated to activate my worry gene but I thought about how tired Evelyn had been lately. She was burning the candle at both ends and I was afraid she'd lit it in the middle as well. I reached for a clean mug for my coffee. "She's been awfully tired lately. That's not like her."

"Aye," said Millie still with a curious smile on her face.

I poured my coffee and took a sip. "Can I help with anything?" I thought if Evelyn wasn't there she might need an extra hand. I could catch up on the rooms later, there were only two.

"If you'd take the fruit bowl in, I'd appreciate it. I'm just finishing up the porridge here and I'll keep it warm. The rest is all there." As I picked up the fruit bowl she had nodded at, she added, "Oh, and please check to see the kettle is plugged in for the water. I don't remember if I did it."

"Sure." I loved the automatic kettles that heated water for tea. You just set it on its metal pad and it heated the water to just the right temperature for tea or any other instant hot beverage. Evelyn had one in each of the guest rooms with a small selection of teas and instant coffee. She'd also gotten some individually wrapped biscotti so guests could enjoy a beverage and snack after our kitchen hours were done.

I set the fruit bowl alongside the breads and rolls and charcuterie board that held an assortment of sliced meats and cheeses. The kettle base was plugged in and I set the pot of water on it making sure the light went on indicating that it was heating. Just as I was about to go back into the kitchen, the Kellys came in.

Linda smiled at me. She was looking a little stronger than when we'd first met. Perhaps all the arrangements for her son were set in order and she was a little less stressed. I noticed though, grief was still engrained in the frown lines and puffiness of her face. My heart hurt for her. She looked at all the food set out on the sideboard and put a hand to her chest.

"My goodness this is all so lovely," she said. "We've never stayed in such a nice bed and breakfast place. Well, actually this is only the second one and the other was back home in the states. Not quite as elegant as this."

I flushed with pleasure and pride, not for me but for Evelyn. It was her doing. "I'm so glad you are feeling comfortable here." I chose my words carefully. I was sure they didn't want me to say they were enjoying their stay. Who could enjoy the constant reminder of why they were here? "Would you like a hot breakfast this morning? Millie is at the stove with some porridge—that's oatmeal for us Americans." That got a little chuckle from Linda and a smile from Patrick. "And I'm sure she wouldn't mind making some eggs and sausage," I added. I had seen that Millie had the eggs and sausage ready if they were ordered. I could help her with that as well.

"Oh, no thank you." Linda shook her head then looked at her husband. "Unless you would like something, Patrick?"

"A little of that porridge might be nice," said Patrick, "I'd like to see if it tastes any different on this side of the pond."

I chuckled. "Let me know. I haven't tried it yet." The couple went to the sideboard and began to help themselves to some of the food there while I went into the kitchen to fetch the porridge.

"All well?" asked Millie. "Do I need to make any eggs yet?"

"No. Patrick would like to try your porridge. He wants to know if it tastes any different on this side of the pond." Millie enjoyed the humor and laughed as she ladled some oatmeal into a bowl and set it on a plate for me to take in. "There's brown sugar, raisins, nuts and a little cinnamon in a shaker on the table if he'd like to fancy it up a bit."

"I'll let him know I said backing into the swinging door to deliver the hot bowl of porridge to the dining room. When I returned to the kitchen, Millie asked me if Thornbury was down yet. "Not yet." I shrugged. "That's odd. He's usually up early. I'll wander around a bit and see if I find him." I didn't say it to Millie but I also wanted to check on Evelyn.

The gathering room and library were empty but when I passed the front windows, I noticed his car was gone. He was off somewhere already. I popped my head into the kitchen to tell Millie I thought he'd left and then continued down the hall to Evelyn's rooms. Just as I was about to knock on the door, it opened and Evelyn clutched her throat at the surprise to see me standing there.

"Oh!" Evelyn said, "I didn't know you were there."

"I was about to knock. Are you feeling okay?" I noticed she looked a bit pale. "Millie said you were a bit under the weather this morning."

"I just had a rough start," she came out into the hall and closed the door behind her. "Maybe cottage pie doesn't agree with me although I can't imagine what would have been in it that I haven't had before."

"Maybe the Guinness," I said as we started down the hall together. "That Guinness does strange things to my tummy." After I said that I wondered why it hadn't affected me then as well.

"I'm okay now," Evelyn said rubbing her stomach a bit. "I guess I got it all out of my system. Is Millie doing okay in the kitchen without me?"

"She's a gem. Got it all handled. Although we're one short at breakfast this morning. Thornbury is missing. Haven't seen him and his car is gone."

"That's odd. He strikes me as a creature of habit since he always has the same breakfast. Well, we'll hold his porridge for a bit but then the kitchen has to close for breakfast."

Evelyn went off to check on Millie and I went to gather my cleaning supplies to freshen the rooms. Today we would change the bed linens for Thornbury. I went off to work in the Kellys' room while I waited for Millie to help me with the sheets for Thornbury's room.

As I remade the bed and lightly dusted around the room, I thought about the remark the Kellys had made to Charles about the seminar James attended. If he was a student, the seminar had to be somewhere in Ireland, probably around Dublin. I wondered if I could find any information on something like that after it had already taken place. I was encouraged when I thought about what people always said about things on the internet. Once it was out there, it was there forever.

I hoped so.

14

Millie found me just as I was coming out of the Kellys' room. She was carrying the fresh linens. "Just in time," I said. "This room is done and we only have Thornbury's to do. I hope he really is gone. I'd hate to surprise him."

"Or be surprised," Millie said. I wondered if she was nervous about my reputation for finding dead bodies. He couldn't possibly be in his room, dead or alive, if his car was gone. I knocked on the door anyway, loud and long.

"I think it's safe," said Millie with a chuckle.

I took out my master key and unlocked the door. Just to be sure I called out, "Professor? Housekeeping!" There was no answer but I looked around the room in dismay. There were clothes strewn about as if he'd dressed or undressed in a hurry. A pair of black pants and a black sweatshirt was draped over the chair at the desk. I checked the desktop to be sure the manuscript wasn't out there again. It wasn't but there was a pile of books obviously checked out of the library from town. Some of them I recognized as donations from our own library. What was he researching?

I didn't want to take time to look through them, not with Millie in the room with me. She didn't need to be implicated in any trouble I might get into while I was investigating. We worked around the room after we changed the linen and folded the clothes we found and placed them on the bed. "I'll run the vacuum," I said as Millie gathered the sheets to take down to the laundry.

"Then I'll be down to wash those if you'll just leave them in the basket down there. I think Evelyn might need you more than I do today if she's not feeling well."

"I think Evelyn will be just fine," said Millie with a wink before she turned and went out the door. How could she be so sure that Evelyn would be okay? Maybe it was her Irish intuition or something. I was her mother though and I wasn't so sure. I started the vacuum.

I had finished sweeping most of the room when the end of the wand suddenly bumped against something on the floor beneath the desk. A box full of little green batteries was plugged into the outlet there. I recognized what it was, a charger for rechargeable batteries. Paul had had one for charging the batteries he used in his flashlight. I used to tease him about being a penny pincher, not wanting to buy new batteries when he needed them. I wondered what Thornbury needed batteries for? Stranger still was the black piece of clothing I picked up that had fallen between the desk and the wall. It was a black ski mask. Curiouser and curiouser. I set the mask on top of the folded clothes on the bed and quickly finished the sweeping. Where was Max, I wondered? He needed to hear about this.

I couldn't find Max but I caught up with Charles as he was painting some new trim around the front door. "Is Max around?" I asked him. He turned to me and I had to laugh. Somehow he had managed to paint the tip of his nose. I rubbed mine thinking he would get the idea that there was something on his but he just looked at me blankly so I had to say, "Charles you are getting too close to your work. You have paint on your nose."

"Oh!" He put his paintbrush down and reached around to his back pocket that had a rag tucked into it. He rubbed at his nose with the rag. "Better?"

"A little," I said grinning at him. "You might need to clean it up better when you're done."

"Thanks. I'll keep that in mind and try not to stick my nose into the paint again." He picked up his brush and dipped it in the small can of paint at his feet. "You were looking for Max, weren't you? He and Finn went into town a bit ago. Finn needed some more flower bulbs and Max said something about checking out the building department to see if he could find out more about the castle and its former owners."

"And you let him get distracted from his work?" I said. "If he goes off investigating this whole mystery of James and Thornbury, you're not going to get any work done."

"He's helped so much already that I'm having to look for more projects to do around here." Charles turned and continued with his painting. "The lodge is pretty close to being all fixed and repaired. I'm going to see what else Evelyn might have up her sleeve for us to do. She always has new ideas."

"She'll keep you busy," I said. "Well, I guess what I have to tell him can wait."

"Was it something I can help with?" Charles asked.

"Just something very curious I found in Thornbury's room this morning."

"What's that?" I had his attention. He turned to me again with the paintbrush dripping paint down his arm. He quickly wiped it with the rag and set the brush on top of the paint can.

"His room was a bit messy and we had to fold some clothes he'd tossed over his chair and around the room. The shirt and sweatpants were black. And then I found a black ski mask under the desk. It had all the makings of an outfit for a burglar."

"That is odd," said Charles still trying to wipe paint from his arm. "I'm sure it will be important to Max." He stopped and frowned. "You know, whoever was in that video was impossible to see. I wonder if he was dressed in black?"

"Could it have been Thornbury?" We looked at each other contemplating the idea. "There was one more thing that may or may not be important."

"What?"

"There was also a charger set up with a set of batteries in it. I wonder what he needed them for?"

"Well, Max has a cleverer mind than I do. We'll see what he has to say when he comes back. Meanwhile, I'd better get this painted before we have too much traffic coming and going here." He picked up the brush and dipped it in the paint. "I'm beginning to have a whole new appreciation for those fellows who maintained our cruise ship. They were constantly painting something."

I left Charles softly whistling while he painted. I loved him. He was such an easy-going guy. Evelyn was blessed to have him. I decided to check up on her before I began my dusting. I also wanted to lightly mop the foyer entrance. It seemed to be showing some footprints from the damp earth outside. I thought maybe it was from the Kellys when they went to the castle but I'd only just noticed them so maybe it was Thornbury or else one of us. I shook my head. One of us was unlikely. We usually used the back door by the kitchen.

Millie and Evelyn were in the kitchen getting lunch ready and making some pastries for afternoon tea. Evelyn said she was doing much better and to stop worrying about her. Millie winked at me again which made me wonder what she was trying to tell me. Was I being too much of a hovering mother? Evelyn was an adult after all. Still, my worry gene kept itching.

I mopped the front foyer so it would have time to dry before our guests came back for tea. I wondered if Thornbury would take tea with us today since he'd skipped breakfast. I had noticed when I cleaned his room that he'd at least had tea sometime last night or this morning since his tea makings were all tossed in the waste can and the wrappers from the biscotti were all on the nightstand. I had replenished all of it and emptied the kettle.

The mopping done and the dusting finished, I

joined the team in the kitchen. Everyone was there except Max. I looked at Finn. "What did you do with Max?"

"I believe Max is out chasing a leprechaun to get his treasure." Finn's eyes twinkled at me as he tried to hide a grin.

"Sure, Finn," I said putting my hands on my hips. "And just where did he see this leprechaun? And is there any hope he will catch him?"

"Well," said Charles with a chuckle, "if anyone could catch a leprechaun and get his gold it would be Max."

"Seriously, you two. What happened to Max?" I hoped they would get to the truth before we went through all the leprechaun tales they could muster.

"Max was still looking for some answers at the building department and the library," said Finn. "He told me to go on without him. He figures to walk home but I don't think he realizes the climb to get here." Finn sat down at the table with the bowl of soup that Millie handed him. "I'll check on him in another hour or two and pick him up before he wearies himself."

"Thank you, Finn," I said.

"I'll be goin' that way soon," said Millie. "I can check on him. Afternoon tea is all ready except for heatin' the water."

I sat down with my cream of mushroom soup and a roll and pondered just what Max may have found that kept him in town.

"You know, Miss Casey," said Finn between spoonfuls of soup, 'it's possible we have a leprechaun digging around the castle. They are known to bury their gold and treasure in strange places."

"Are you serious?" I asked. He said it so matter-of-factly that it seemed a reasonable truth.

"No," said Millie. "Finn is just hopeful that the stories of leprechaun gold are true. Truth be told though the little fellas are shoemakers. Now when did you ever hear of a rich shoemaker?"

I looked from one to the other. Who was putting me on? One or both? I decided to play along. I broke my roll in half to butter a piece and said, "I hear tell that you can find the pot of gold at the end of a rainbow. Trouble is you need sunshine and rain together to have a rainbow and I have yet to see that happen here in Ireland."

Charles lost it and almost spewed soup as he couldn't contain a good laugh. "I think she's on to you Finn," he said and took a drink of water.

Millie finally shared the folklore she knew about leprechauns and the stories that people claimed were true. I found it most interesting though when she said that they were thought to be from the days when Ireland had an Irish deity, Lugh, god of the sun and of arts and crafts. With the rise of Christianity, Lugh's importance diminished. He became a shoe-making folklore character known as Lugh-chromain. By the time the tales of merry making and green hats and little characters that disappeared were done, we were finished with lunch. I helped Evelyn clean up from our meal and told her to call me when she was ready to set out the tea things. I was eager to find a little more information myself but about castles and jewels and a man named Thornbury.

I made a little coffee and snitched one of the pastries from the afternoon tea tray to take back to my room. I sat on the sofa and put my feet up on the ottoman. Beside me were the books I'd taken from our library when I looked for information about Shamrock Castle. I set the large heavy one on my lap and opened it. I thumbed through pictures of castles and marveled at how they could all be so different. Architecture nowadays was too bland and certainly did not have the same kind of detail that I saw in many of the castles. Those that had interior pictures were even more fascinating.

When I decided it was a waste of time going through the book page by page, I flipped it over and opened it from the back. To my relief there was an index and it was organized by area and county, then city. I found Dingle on the list and there was Castle Glas, the name of Shamrock before the new owners had changed it. It was a few more pages toward the front of the book and when I got to the place it should be, I was confused. The page numbers didn't make sense. I realized that someone had neatly cut out the two pages that held the information about the castle. That was disappointing. Who would do that? Why damage a perfectly good book like that?

Setting the castle book aside, I sipped some coffee and finished off the lovely bit of pastry that was filled with nuts and had a sweet honey flavored topping. I wiped my hands on a napkin and reached for the book about the crown jewels. I was sure it was a novel when I first picked it up in the library but now I realized it was non-fiction. I knew I wouldn't have time to read through it carefully this afternoon so I began to skim the pages and read bits and pieces of the information there. It wasn't a whole lot different from the story Finn had told us, just a lot more detailed and went into the backgrounds of the major people involved in the theft and disappearance of the jewels. Francis Shackleton and his relationship to the more famous brother, Ernest, had a whole chapter devoted to him as did Sir Arthur Vicars, who was the keeper of the keys to the safe in the library of Dublin Castle where the jewels were stored.

As I read through the biographical material on Vicars, I found that in 1921 he was killed by the IRA while living in a country estate in Kerry County. I whipped out my phone and did a Google search on it for Dingle and Kerry County. Sure enough. Dingle was in Kerry County. Could there be a connection? Could the castle or the lodge have been where he lived? How old was the lodge? So many questions.

Where was Max? I could use some help searching this out.

I looked at my watch. It was almost time for tea. I marked my spot in the book about the jewels and gathered my plate and cup to take to the kitchen. When I entered, I saw Max sitting at the table with Charles. They both looked up at me. "I see you found your way home," I said setting my things in the sink. "Finn told me you were out chasing leprechauns."

Max smiled. "You might say that. Luckily he also knew what kind of an uphill walk it was from town back to the lodge and he came and picked me up on the side of the road before I was completely done in. Guess I'm not in as good a shape as I thought."

I walked over to the table and took a seat. "So, did you find out anything interesting?"

"Indeed I did," said Max. He looked from me to Charles. "But I understand my little sleuth found some interesting clothing items as well."

"I wasn't sleuthing," I said trying to sound indignant. "I was just doing my job, cleaning the room and Millie was there too."

"So you work as a sleuthing team now?" Max said with his Columbo eyebrow raised.

"We were changing the bed linen," I retorted. I didn't want him thinking I had pulled Millie into all our investigating. "We found the clothes together but later, when I was vacuuming, I found the really strange item. A black ski mask."

"Our Professor Thornbury is raising more questions than we have answers for. He—" Evelyn came in and put a finger to her lips to silence Max.

"The professor is taking tea with us and the Kellys have just arrived with him. Save your talk for later." She picked up the tray of pastries and scones and took the wrapping off of it. "Mom can you grab the butter and jam? Oh, and the cream?"

"Sure, honey." I rose quickly and gathered everything together on another tray to take in. When I entered the dining room, Thornbury was seated with his cup of tea already poured. He looked like he needed a cup of tea or maybe something stronger. Dark circles rimmed his eyes and his hair was slightly askew. Nothing like the demeanor of the prim and proper professor he usually portrayed. What had him out of sorts? And where had he been all this time? I decided to join in on afternoon tea. Perhaps I'd get a hint of his activities. Besides, I could use another one of those nutty honey topped pastries.

15

Unfortunately the only thing I learned from afternoon tea was that the Kellys had finally been allowed to see James. The autopsy had been done and they were holding his body until the repatriation provider finished gathering the paperwork and making the arrangements to fly him home. I had a little idea of what they were going through. Somehow no matter how much you tell yourself that your loved one has died it's not real until you see them. I couldn't imagine how people who didn't have that opportunity for a last goodbye dealt with the loss.

Thornbury sat quietly. I couldn't tell if he was listening to the Kellys talk of their day's activities or if he had just removed himself mentally from the whole conversation. He went back to the sideboard several times. I guessed that he had missed lunch. Finally, I ventured a question to bring him into the conversation.

"How was your day so far, Professor Thornbury?" He didn't seem to hear me at first and then gave a look of surprise as if he hadn't recognized that I was speaking to him.

"Unproductive. Very unproductive," he said. "If you'll excuse me, I have work to do." He rose abruptly with a small plate of sandwiches and left the room. I could hear his feet trudge up the wooden stairs to his room.

I cleared the dishes from tea when the Kellys were finished. Millie had already gone home for the day and I assumed Evelyn was ensconced in her office again. I was beginning to think she spent more time at that computer than she should but I was being too motherly again. I decided not to mention it. What I really wanted to do though was find Max. I was more curious than a cat about what he'd found in town.

When I couldn't find him around the lodge, I grabbed my heavy sweater, took the dog leash off the hook and called for Allie. She roused herself slowly from a spot in the sun in the library where she'd snoozed the afternoon away. Once she saw the leash though, she was eager to go. There was no way I would walk her without the leash. Her urge to herd the sea gulls was still strong and I wasn't about to chase after her again. There was a bit of a cool wind and I was glad I'd worn the sweater. We started up the drive toward the castle. Men's voices caught my attention and instead of walking through the meadow area, we kept to the driveway and followed the sound.

Halfway up the drive, I saw our three industrious guys with shovels and a wheelbarrow. There was quite a pile of gravel blocking part of the drive and they were filling the wheelbarrow and dumping it along the edge of the harder beaten path of stone we drove on.

"You all look like you're having fun," I said facetiously. Charles, Max and Finn looked harried and were sweating despite the cool weather. They all leaned on their shovels for a moment and wiped their foreheads.

"Fun?" said Max. "If this is fun, why don't you join us?" He offered his shovel to me.

"Oh no thanks," I said lightly, "I wouldn't want to take away from your fun."

Allie had extended her leash as far as she could trying to snuggle up to Finn. He finally moved toward her and playfully ran his fingers over her ears. She lapped up the attention.

"Did you need something?" Charles asked. "We really need to get this pile moved before our guests have to use the driveway. We're trying to shore up the sides of the road where it gets soft from the rain. It looks like someone has already driven through the soft spot last night."

"We were just out walking and heard the grunts and groans," I said with a laugh. I reined Allie in closer. "Just wondered what was going on. I'll see you later." I turned and waved a hand over my head. "Carry on, gentlemen."

Max was going to be exhausted tonight. There wouldn't be much help from him with searching for information on our subjects. I refilled Allie's water bowl in the kitchen foyer and fought the urge to check on what Evelyn had in the oven that smelled so good. When had she learned to be such a good cook? Certainly not on the cruise ship.

A glance at my watch told me I had a little time to do some more work on my laptop or skimming through the crown jewels book or, I suddenly remembered, the letters. I hadn't looked through the letters yet. I picked up my pace as I headed to my room. That was my project for the afternoon.

As I passed the door to Charles and Evelyn's rooms, it opened. "Mom?" Evelyn stood in the doorway looking forlorn. "I thought I heard you." I immediately went to her.

"Honey, what's wrong?"

She moved back from the doorway a bit and said, "Can you come in for a few minutes?"

"Of course." I walked in and saw a box of tissues on the end table with several used ones piled next to it. What was going on? She was obviously upset about something. I turned and Evelyn rushed into my arms.

"Oh, Mom," she started sobbing. "What am I going to do?"

"Do? About what? What is it?" I caressed her head like I did when she was a little girl and had fallen and hurt herself. My heart was pounding. What could be wrong that she was so upset? Had the company fired us all? Was the bed and breakfast about to close before it even got going?

Evelyn sank onto the sofa and grabbed another tissue. She reached in her pocket and pulled out a white stick and held it out to me. I took it but didn't understand. There was a little window with two lines in it. "What is this?" I asked but in the back of my head a little voice was calling me a dummy.

"It's a home pregnancy test," she said quietly. "It's positive." Her eyes brimmed over with tears and she dabbed at them with a tissue. "Millie kept telling me she thought that was what was wrong with me but I didn't want to believe her. When I went into town to pick up some groceries I bought a pregnancy test as well. Since Charles had work to do all afternoon, I thought it was a good time to take it." She gave me a forlorn look. "What am I going to do?"

A part of me wanted to rejoice with the thought of being a Grandmother and yet my heart broke for my daughter who was obviously upset by the news. I tried to stay calm. The best way to handle this was with a hug. I sat down next to her and cradled her head on my shoulder. I said nothing and waited for her to figure it out. I had confidence that once she thought about it, the prospect of becoming a mother wouldn't seem so daunting.

She sat up and reached for another tissue. "I don't know how to tell Charles. We just started this business. How can we bring a child into this world when we haven't figured it all out yet."

I tried not to chuckle. No one has ever figured out their world before a child comes along no matter how much planning was involved. "Honey, you will be just fine. A baby will be a little more work, yes, but you and Charles are very organized and the B&B is coming together so nicely that a baby will just be a pleasant adjustment to everything else."

"No, you don't understand," said Evelyn. She took a deep breath. I could see her begin to get control again. "Charles was adamant about not starting a family until we were up and running for a year. It's only been a couple of months and we've just started with guests. I don't know what he's going to say. I didn't do this on purpose. I don't know how it happened."

I had to smile at that. "Birth control is not a hundred percent effective. And if God wants this child in your life, then all the birth control in the world is not going to stop him from giving you a baby." I brushed some wayward strands of hair from her cheek. "Charles loves you deeply. I see that every day in the way he looks at you and touches you. He's a kind loving person. He will accept the news with grace and, I'm certain, a little eagerness to share in this blessed event."

We sat quietly for a few minutes. I could almost hear Evelyn thinking. She sat up straighter. "The pregnancy test might be wrong. How accurate are these things anyway?"

I didn't want to argue that point with her but home pregnancy tests had come a long ways since my day. "Well, you could take another one or actually go in to see a doctor and have them run a test in the office." I thought for a moment. "How far along do you think you are?"

"I don't know I just realized I missed a period but it could have been two. I've been so busy I haven't thought about it."

"You would need to see a doctor anyway to start your prenatal visits if you are pregnant. Do you know anyone in town?"

"No, I haven't had time to establish a doctor yet," Evelyn said wearily. "I'm sure Millie will know someone. I'll give her a call."

"Good idea," I said and patted her knee. "Now let's think about something else for a bit—like that wonderful smell in the kitchen. Another casserole? Do we need to check on it? I have a feeling those guys are going to be really hungry by dinner. And then after that they're going to need a lot of TLC for all their aches and pains."

Evelyn smiled. "Charles said he's found muscles he didn't know he had with all the maintenance work he's done since we've been here." She rose from the sofa and gathered all the used tissues. "Okay, I have a plan and we have dinner to get on the table." She bent down and kissed me on the cheek. "Thanks for listening, Mom."

"Anytime, honey, anytime."

16

Tuesday morning dawned with the promise of a beautiful spring day. I woke with a smile on my face. I was going to be a grandma! The trouble was I couldn't tell anyone yet. Evelyn had made me promise not to say anything until she was certain and she had told Charles. The only other one who knew was Millie because she had figured it out long before I ever suspected. At least I could share it with her.

Max had been too tired the night before to talk about his discoveries when he went into town to the building department and the library to research the castle and its previous owners. He had gone straight to bed after dinner. We planned on an evening of brainstorming and researching tonight and in the meantime, keeping an eye on Thornbury who seemed to be getting even more out of sorts as time went on.

Since Evelyn was having a rough start again to her morning, I offered to help Millie with getting breakfast and then go up to refresh the rooms. As I set out trays of fruit and rolls on the sideboard, Linda came in. She went to the coffee pot and poured coffee into one of the pretty colorful mugs that Evelyn had purchased for the lodge. She took a sip and sighed heavily.

"Casey, did you ever wish you could go back and redo something?" She shook her head a bit. "I just think that if we hadn't lent James the money for that seminar he wanted to attend, things may have been different. I'm convinced that was the catalyst for his venture to the castle."

"What do you mean?" I poured myself a cup of coffee and sat next to her at the table. I had the feeling this might be helpful information.

"He needed money to travel to Belfast for the seminar on Irish folklore. He said it was given by a prominent professor in Irish history and he felt it would lend to his studies. He just seemed to change after that." She shrugged and sipped her coffee.

"Change how?" I asked. Making a mental note that the seminar was in Belfast.

"When we went to get his things from school, his professors at the college told us he was cutting classes and not turning in assignments. Something that was out of character for him." A tear formed and trickled down her cheek. She wiped it away quickly. "I just wish we'd made a different decision, told him we didn't have the money. It seemed the right thing to do at the time. He was so excited about the opportunity."

"There are many things in life that, had I opportunity, I might have done differently but unfortunately there's no going back." I ached for her. She didn't need to add guilt to the grief she carried. "I'm sorry for how this all ended but you can't blame yourself. Our children make their own decisions. He would have found a way to get to that seminar without your help if he genuinely wanted to be there."

She slowly nodded. "I guess you're right. I just wish—" She stopped mid-sentence as Patrick came into the room.

"Are you beating yourself up again about James?" he said rather coldly. "I told you it doesn't matter. What's done is done." He went over and poured himself a cup of coffee and grabbed a plate. His grief seemed to have made him angry and distant but then I didn't really know him before all this had happened. Maybe that was his nature.

I rose quickly. I felt it was my time to exit. The tension between the two of them permeated the room. "Would either of you like anything hot this morning?" I asked before I went into the kitchen.

Linda shook her head and Patrick looked from her to me and said, "No, thank you." He walked to the table and pulled out the chair across from Linda and sat down. I took my leave.

As I entered the kitchen, Millie turned to me to see if she needed to cook something. I shook my head. "They're fine. Nothing hot." I set my cup in the sink. "Thornbury still hasn't shown up. I'll go check and see if his car is still here."

"I have some porridge ready if he's around," Millie said as she put a lid on a pot and set it to the back of the stove.

I looked through one of the gathering room windows that gave a view of the driveway and the space where guests could park. Thornbury was out there with the trunk lid up. He seemed to be fidgeting with something in the trunk. I decided to check it out.

He was so intent upon what he was doing that he didn't hear me approach. As I neared the back of the car, I could see that he was holding one end of a long metal stick that had some sort of a metal box attached to it. My guess was that he was putting batteries in something as one fell out and rolled toward me. I bent down to pick it up but he was quick to grab it and toss it into the trunk while closing it quickly so I couldn't see what was in there.

"What do you need, Ms. Stengel?" He asked with a scowl on his face.

"I saw you out here and wondered if you would like breakfast before you begin your day," I said as sweetly as I could.

He looked to the closed trunk and back at me. "Ah, well, ah," he stuttered. "I guess I should. Perhaps starting my day with a bit of porridge will bring me better results."

"Millie has it ready for you." I turned and he followed me back into the lodge.

"I'll be in as soon as I wash up." Thornbury disappeared into the powder room down the hall.

"The professor will take his porridge now," I told Millie. She nodded her head and got a bowl from the cupboard. "I'll go check to be sure the water is hot for tea."

The Kellys were still sipping coffee and munching on toast. Both were very quiet. I saw that the water was hot and the tea bags were all set in place. Millie brought the porridge in just as Thornbury brushed past me on his way into the dining room. I hustled off to refresh rooms while our guests were still having breakfast.

The Kellys' room just required a refreshing of towels and making the bed. They would be checking out in the morning provided there was no hold up with the repatriation of James. I finished quickly and went on to Thornbury's room. It was much neater than the previous day and there was nothing unusual to grab my attention. I didn't linger. He wasn't pleased with me glancing in his car's trunk. I didn't want him coming in while I was there. What was that thing he was working on? Max and I needed some time together to figure out the puzzle pieces we each had found. It was sure to come together soon.

On my way to the laundry to toss the towels into the washer, I met Evelyn. She looked nervous but sounded excited if that made any sense. "Mom, can you help Millie with afternoon tea? I managed to get an appointment with the OB/GYN in town for this afternoon. Millie knows his nurse and they had a cancellation so she scheduled me into the spot."

"Sure, honey. Millie and I can handle the tea. I'll get my chores done quickly and have plenty of time to help make sandwiches."

"Millie is already mixing up the scones to bake and she brought some other little pastries from the bakery in town."

I wrapped one of her arms in mine and walked her back to her door. "See how well organized you are. You've got this, girl. Whatever the result of your doctor's visit, you'll be just fine."

"I only 'got this' because of you and Millie. Without you two I wouldn't be able to do anything."

"A wise person once said, 'sometimes you need a hand and sometimes you give a hand.' We all need to help each other."

Evelyn laughed. "Was that wise person you?"

"Not this time but I'm sure I'll find some other gems of wisdom to share along the way." I patted her arm and went off to the laundry, mentally organizing what I needed to do to be able to help with tea and finish my chores.

As I checked the library and gathering room, I passed Allie who'd found another spot of sun to sleep in. She lifted her head and her tail slapped against the floor expectantly. "Not right now, girl. Maybe later." I didn't dare mention the word 'walk' or she would have been up like a shot and running circles. I chuckled. There were several words she'd finally learned although the commands were not learned as well as the fun things like a walk. She would be good company for the little one that I was positive would come in another six or seven months.

I picked up a few books and set them back in their place on the shelf. Suddenly Allie brushed against my legs and growled. I turned to see Thornbury at the door. He scowled at Allie and then looked up at me. "I can't seem to find your daughter.

I will require another night or two here to finish my work. Is my room available?"

I hushed Allie and made her sit but the hair on her back was still raised and her eyes never strayed from Thornbury. "We don't have anyone else booked for your room for a while so if you need a few more nights, I believe that can easily be arranged. Evelyn will be back later this afternoon. I'll let her know."

He nodded at me, turned on his heel and left without so much as a "thank you." Where had the manners gone that were so evident when he first arrived? His demeanor had changed as days went on. Whatever he was searching for was obviously not within his grasp and was fraying his nerves.

We fixed lunch for the men and then began the preparations for tea. Evelyn had already sliced the cucumbers for Max's favorite little tea sandwiches. I smiled as I remembered big manly Max enjoying the delicate treats. We found egg salad and chicken salad that Evelyn had prepared and carefully spread them on our cutout bread pieces. When we were done, we stood back and admired our handiwork before covering it tightly to keep the bread from drying out then set them in the refrigerator.

As I arranged the pastries on a tray, Millie baked the scones. She set a baking sheet in the oven and set the timer. When she turned she asked, "So will you be having a grand time as Nana?" Her smile spread to her brown eyes that twinkled as if there were flecks of gold there.

"Does it show?" I laughed. "Expectant mothers are supposed to glow. Do grandmas as well?"

Millie gave me a hug. "I hope our girl realizes how lucky she is." She pulled back and I saw the glistening of tears in her eyes. "Finn and I are not so fortunate. There will be no little ones for us." She took a deep breath and smiled again. "So I will love the little ones that others have and enjoy watching them grow."

"Oh, Millie, I'm so sorry." I had no idea. I knew they had no children but I thought they were just waiting for the right time. "Is there no chance for adoption? There are so many children in the world who need a good home."

"Finn is not ready to consider that yet." She turned and peeked into the oven to see if the scones were done. "I was hopin' when Evelyn has the baby, maybe he will change his mind."

"Your Finn is a fine man. He will come around."

The timer rang and Millie took the scones from the oven. I looked at my watch. Afternoon tea was about to begin. I knew the Kellys would be there for tea but would Thornbury? I began to take the trays into the dining room and set up the sideboard with the kettle of water and the tea assortment. Millie came in with the plate of scones that looked perfectly delicious and smelled wonderful as they were fresh from the oven. I hoped there were some left for the men to enjoy as well.

We had just finished setting up when Linda and Patrick came in. They had been on a walk and shed their heavy sweaters and hung them on the backs of their chairs. Linda surveyed the sideboard. "I am going to miss this. It's been a real treat. Thank you all." She looked from me to Millie. "You have been so kind and you've made this difficult trip a little easier for us." Her eyes glistened.

Patrick wasted no time in filling his plate with sandwiches and scones. "It has been nice to enjoy this each day," he said seating himself at the table. "Linda, maybe we could make this a habit at home." He winked at her. I was glad to see that his mood was a little lighter this afternoon.

"Has everything gone well with repatriation?" I asked.

"The provider has it all in hand and James will be on his way home the same time we will," Patrick said as he poured his tea from the little teapot he'd filled at the sideboard. "His sister is making arrangements back home for the memorial service. At least we don't have to face all of that when we get back."

"I didn't know James had a sister," I said. Millie had gone back into the kitchen but I helped myself to some tea and decided to join them. "Is she older? Younger?"

"She's older and married." Linda wiped a bit of jam from her mouth. "She's expecting our first grandchild in a couple of months." She smiled and for the first time I saw a flicker of joy in her face.

"Ah, something good to look forward to," I said nodding my head. Oh how I wanted to share my news but I knew I couldn't.

At that moment, Thornbury strode into the room. He appeared less frazzled than he had at yesterday's tea. His hair was combed back and his clothes looked fresh. He helped himself to a plate of sandwiches and poured his pot of tea before seating himself at the other end of the table from us.

"Good afternoon, Professor," I said as he adjusted his napkin in his lap.

"Afternoon," he replied with a curt nod.

A look passed between Linda and Patrick. She took a sip of tea and then turned to Thornbury. "Professor Thornbury, did I hear that you taught at the University College Dublin?"

Thornbury paused with his teacup halfway to his lips. For a moment I wasn't sure he would acknowledge the question let alone answer it. He took a sip and slowly settled his cup back into the saucer. Without looking directly at Linda he said, "I was there at one time but I've taken a leave to further study and do research for my own project."

"Oh," said Linda sadly, "I had hoped you might have known our son. He studied there."

Thornbury swallowed the bite of sandwich in his mouth and slowly shook his head. "I'm afraid I wouldn't be acquainted with the young man. I've been gone from the university for quite some time now."

"It's just that in one of the letters from James, he'd mentioned a professor and I thought your name sounded similar to the one in the letter."

Slowly Thornbury lowered his hands to the table and placed one on each side of his plate. For the first time he looked directly at Linda, a slight frown on his face. "Madam, I am sorry for your loss but I did not know your son." He pushed back from the table and rose. "Now, if you will excuse me."

Linda opened her mouth as if to pose another question but Patrick put a hand on her arm. "Let it go Linda."

Her mouth formed a "But. . ." Nothing came out. She lifted her cup with two shaky hands and drained its contents.

"Can I get you another pot of tea?" I asked. She looked like she could use something more.

She put an elbow on the table and rested her forehead in her hand. "Yes, thank you, Casey. I could use another cup." I made my way to the sideboard and hoped there was still enough hot water in the kettle.

Patrick stood and put a hand on Linda's shoulder. "I'm going to the library to read. I'll be there if you need me." Linda nodded.

I sat down with the pot of tea that was steeping. Linda appeared a bit shaken. Was it from the way Thornbury had so rudely answered her? What had she expected from him? Another connection somehow to her son? Something to keep him alive in her mind and heart?

I posed the question gently. “What made you think Thornbury might know James?”

She lifted her head and put her hands around her empty cup. “I could swear that the name of the professor James wrote about when he asked for the seminar money was Thornbury. It’s an unusual name. I think that’s why it stuck.” She shook her head. “I guess I was wrong.” She sighed deeply. “And Patrick is right. I need to let it go. Nothing is going to bring James back and what’s done is done. I can’t change anything with regrets.”

I poured tea into her cup. “It’s so very difficult to let go all at once. I know. When my husband died, I walked around talking to him all day even though he wasn’t there anymore. I can’t imagine what it must be like to lose a child.” I drank what was left of my tea. It had grown cold as I’d watched the drama unfold before me. “Charles and Finn just installed a new bench under the tree near the flower garden at the side of the lodge. Why don’t you take your tea out there and enjoy the sunshine and flowers and relax a bit while you can? I’ll put the pot and a couple little pastries on a tray for you.”

She gave me a crooked smile. “That sounds lovely, Casey. Thank you.” In a few minutes, she was on her way to the garden. I whispered a little prayer for God to put his arms around her and comfort her.

By the time I cleared everything from the sideboard in the dining room, the men had also finished their afternoon coffee break, although Finn’s was tea. The extra sandwiches and pastries Millie had set aside for them were consumed. Except for a few small plates there wasn’t much left to clean up.

“Why don’t you go ahead home, Millie?” I said as I rinsed the plates from the dining room. “I can wash the rest of these.”

"If you don't mind," she said taking off her kitchen apron. "Evelyn texted to say she was still at the doctor's office. Someone delivered a baby and put all the appointments behind. She suggested we all go out for dinner tonight. The fellas seemed to like the idea—something about a round of Guinness." She chuckled. "I'll go home with Finn and change into something else and come back so we can all leave together. And I want to hear the news." She smiled and winked. "I'm sure it will be good news. I can't wait."

I wanted to hear the news as well. The question was, when would Evelyn give the news to Charles? Even if it was a swing and a miss, she was going to have to tell him. I set the last dish in the washer and started it. I wanted to do some online searching for Thornbury but not until after I checked on my Dodgers. That information would be easier to find than a professor who may or may not actually be a professor or who may or may not have taught a seminar on Irish folklore.

17

The Dodgers were on a streak. Their website said they'd won the last three of four. I made a note to ask Charles to record another game for Max and me to watch. Hopefully Charles would catch a game that was a winner. That done, I turned to searching for the seminar that may have enticed James onto a disastrous path. It didn't take long to find it. I was getting good at loading the right words into a search box.

Even though the seminar had been months ago, the advertising for it was still online. I saw the price and calculated that it was a little more than five hundred US dollars for the seminar alone. It was a two day affair so James would have needed a little extra for accommodations and food and transportation to Belfast from Dublin. Definitely not in a student's budget.

Scrolling through the outline of the proposed content, revealed that it covered a little of Irish history but its main thrust was the mystery of the stolen Irish crown jewels. As I dove into more of the details, I felt like I'd seen this information outlined before. I glanced over at the book resting on the coffee table that I'd taken from our library, *The Case Of The Irish Crown Jewels*. I opened it to the table of contents. It matched the outline of the seminar and covered all the main characters and events. The only difference was that the last subject of the seminar posed the question, "Where are the jewels now?"

When I got to the bottom of the page I suddenly realized I had passed over a picture along the way. I scrolled back up and sure enough, there looking his scowling self was Professor Thornbury. His skeletal face with the large nose and prominent cheekbones were unmistakable. The hair was a bit different. There was a lot more gray in it which confirmed my suspicion that his dark hair was dyed. The short biographical information stated that he was a professor emeritus from University College Dublin and listed several universities in the States where he'd taught. There was a quote from some magazine I assumed was professional that said he was a leading expert on the folklore of Ireland and especially the unsolved mystery of the crown jewels.

I sat back and pondered for a moment. Max said he hadn't been listed on the faculty at Dublin. Had he retired that long ago? He was a bit young to retire but maybe he'd made enough money to take an early retirement. There must be some way to find out. I found the website for the university and searched down the page for phone numbers. I found one that looked promising and picked up my cell phone. Nothing ventured, nothing gained.

After getting switched to several different extensions, I finally got a gentleman who identified himself as the director of Irish studies. "How can I be of assistance?" he asked with a beautiful Irish lilt to his deep voice.

"I'm looking for a professor of Irish history and folklore and I wondered if he taught at the University at any time?" I asked nervously.

"Yes? And who might that be?"

"A Professor Thornbury."

There was a long pause followed by a deep breath that was released in a hiss of air. "Madam, we have no Professor Thornbury associated with our university. We have never had a Professor Thornbury associated with our university. His seminars are not associated with our university in any way. If you have encountered any monetary difficulties with said seminars, I suggest you contact the authorities. I'm sorry that's all the information I have." There was a click on the line and he was gone.

I stared at my phone for a moment. Nothing. Nada. No Thornbury ever. I looked again at the information page of the seminar, at his credits. Should I try to contact the other universities he claimed to be associated with in the States? I shook my head. I seriously doubted he was a professor at any of those schools either.

So who is Thornbury? Is that even his real name? I looked at the outline of the seminar again and picked up *The Case Of The Irish Crown Jewels* to check the table of contents again. Yes, it was exactly like the seminar outline. I went to the title page and found the name of the author. A Daniel Mahone had written the book and it had a foreword written by—Roger Callahan! Was I hitting it out of the park? Or was this just a foul ball that would send me back to the batter's box? I hoped it wasn't a swing and a miss.

There was a soft knock on the door and it opened a crack. "Mom? Can I come in?"

Evelyn was back. "Of course!" I answered eagerly.

She closed the door behind her. When she turned to face me I couldn't tell whether she was happy or not. I tried to wait patiently but my heart was racing and I could barely contain myself. "Well?" I asked.

A smile crept across her face. She reached in her pocket and pulled out a tiny pair of socks. "Here Grandma, I think you'll enjoy dressing up your little grandbaby."

I rushed to her and put my arms around her. After a good hug, I held her away from me a bit and searched her face. "Are you okay with this?"

She nodded. "I don't have time to tell you all that the doctor said but she spent a good deal of time telling me about what to expect and what limitations I might have but, bottom line, she didn't see any reason I couldn't manage a pregnancy and a baby and a B&B as well." Her smile broadened. "She was very encouraging."

"Have you told Charles yet?"

"No, and you and Millie need to keep this a secret until I do." She put a hand on the doorknob. "I'm going to wait until Thursday when we have the day together to tell him. We'll have more time to talk about it without distractions." She smiled. "But I think he'll be excited too." She opened the door. "Now, I have to change clothes for dinner. It's getting cold out there."

The door closed and I did a little happy dance. I looked at the little pair of baby socks in my hand and then held them to my chest. A grandma! I was going to be a grandma. It was as exciting as the day I discovered I was pregnant with Evelyn. I closed my eyes and said a little prayer of thanks and then tucked the socks away in my nightstand where I could take them out and hold them each night before I went to sleep. I hurried to dress for dinner but as I brushed my hair and looked in the mirror, I wondered how I could keep the secret. It seemed to be written all over my face. Maybe I could explain it away as excitement of finding out more about Thornbury.

Max stopped by my door just as I was gathering my warm jacket. I had tossed on a sweater as an added layer but I figured the jacket would be extra insurance. This Florida girl got an Irish chill in the cooler evenings. I smiled up at him as I waved an appraising hand up and down. "So this is my date for the night?"

"Something like that," he said. "I wanted to see if it was okay with you to drive on our own to Fungie's. The young people can spend the evening enjoying their Guinness but you and I need to call it an early evening and get together to exchange our information. We haven't had a chance yet and I think we need to." He raised an eyebrow.

"Sounds good to me. I found out a few more things about Thornbury this afternoon. I've been dying to share." He helped me into my jacket. Well, there, I thought. Now hopefully he will think the twinkle in my eye is because of the information I have about the professor rather than the secret that was swelling my heart with anticipation.

Dinner was delightful. Max ordered Bangers and Mash which was Irish pork sausages with creamy mashed potatoes and a side of veggies. He must have liked it. It disappeared quickly. I ordered traditional fish and chips which was way more than I could eat but Charles and Max helped me out with it. There was a moment of pause when drinks were ordered but my clever daughter said she was a bit chilled and a pot of hot tea sounded better. I seconded the request and gave the same reason. I didn't want Guinness anyway.

Max and I left the youngsters to their desserts and drinks and we started back to the lodge. We were halfway home when he glanced at me and said, "I know."

I gave him a startled look. "You know? Know what?"

He chuckled. "I know that you're going to be a grandma in a few months."

I gasped. "How did you know that? Who told you?"

"Millie told Finn and Finn told me. Quite the secret, huh?"

"Oh no," I whined. "I hope he didn't tell Charles. That's something that Evelyn needs to do and she wants it to be a special time when she and Charles are alone on Thursday."

"Finn swore me to secrecy," He put a hand to his heart and then held it up in the air, palm out flat. "So how do you feel about it?"

"I was a little concerned for Evelyn at first. She seemed really upset at the prospect since they hadn't planned to start a family yet." I caught a little reflection of my face in the side window. I had that smile again. "Bless that doctor in town. She seems to have convinced Evelyn that everything will work out fine. Now we just have to hope that Evelyn convinces Charles." I turned to Max. "I think he'll be fine. That boy loves her so much, nothing is going to damage that and a baby might even bring them closer if that's possible."

"I agree," Max said as he pulled the car into his parking spot at the lodge. "He's a fine young man."

Max got out and before I could even get my jacket and purse in hand, he had the door open for me. My, what a gentleman tonight. I reached up and brushed his cheek with my hand. "Thanks."

I made some coffee and took it to Max's room. He had picked up my laptop and wanted me to join him there. I suspected it was because his room would be papered with sticky notes each with a clue or bit of information that we had gathered. It was his mode of operation when he was deep into an investigation. He opened the door when I knocked with my foot. Sure enough, I set down the coffee on the writing table and saw the spot which had held a pretty print of the Dingle Harbor was empty and the print propped against the wall on the floor. In its place were at least fifty little sticky notes arranged in various columns according to some sort of organization only Max could know.

I poured our coffee and together we studied the wall.

"Now," said Max, taking a pad of sticky notes and a pen in hand. "tell me what you've learned since we last talked."

I listed the clothes we'd found and the ski mask as well as the battery charger. "Oh, and I think I know where those batteries went," I added. I told Max about seeing the long stick and box in the trunk of Thornbury's car and the battery that he'd dropped as he seemed to be loading them into the box at the end of the stick.

"Did one end have like a flat disk on it?" he asked. He made a circle with his hands.

"A disk?" I thought about what I'd seen. "I couldn't tell you. I only saw the end that was sticking out where he was putting the batteries."

"Uh huh," Max grunted. He wrote it down and placed it in a column that contained notes about the video from the trail camera. He stepped back and cupped a hand under his chin as he studied the wall. I saw that he'd written *metal detector* and a question mark on the new sticky note.

"And I did some research about that seminar that James attended The Kellys are certain that's what prompted James to visit the castle."

Max turned to me with a grin. "So my little sleuth has been very busy." He reached for his coffee cup and blew across it before taking a sip.

"I wish you'd stop calling me that," I said a bit indignantly. "I consider it more investigating than sleuthing. Somehow sleuthing sounds underhanded."

"Point taken," Max said as he set his coffee down and picked up his pen and notepad again. "So, what did your *investigation* reveal?"

I gave him a look to let him know I caught the inflection in his voice. "Linda said she thought the name of the seminar professor was Thornbury but she wasn't sure. That sent me on a search for a seminar on Irish history and folklore in Belfast and it popped up quickly. I scrolled through it and found a picture of Thornbury and a list of his accreditations."

"Ah," said Max as he noted the information and put the sticky note in a column that was obviously for information on Thornbury.

"The thing is, it said he was a professor at University College Dublin but he told the Kellys he'd taken a leave of absence quite some time ago when they asked if he knew their son. So, I called the university and got put through to the department of Irish history." Max turned and raised that Columbo eyebrow of his while he squinted with the other. "The department head told me that there was no Thornbury ever associated with the university and the university had no connection to his seminars." Max was writing another note. "Furthermore, he said if I was having a monetary problem with the seminar, he couldn't help me. I should contact the authorities."

Max stuck a couple more notes under Thornbury.

"The other thing I found about the seminar," I continued as Max stood back and continued to study the sticky notes, "was that the seminar outline matched the table of contents in a book I found in our library about the theft of the crown jewels." Max turned his attention to me. "They both list the facts about the case and then give biographies of the major people involved. The seminar though ends with the question, 'Where are the jewels now?'"

"What's the name of this book?" Max readied his pen and sticky note.

"*The Case Of The Irish Crown Jewels*. It was

written by a Daniel Mahone and there was a foreword by Peter Callahan."

Max stopped writing and quickly looked up at me. "Peter Callahan? You're sure?"

"Yes." I nodded. Hadn't I told him about the manuscript I'd seen? I looked up at his Thornbury column. Sure enough, it was there. And next to it was another column that was labeled "Peter Callahan." What had Max found?

18

Peter Callahan. What was so important about Peter Callahan that Max had created a whole new column for him? I squinted as I tried to read his notes. I gave up. Only Max could read his shorthand. "Why is Peter Callahan important?" I said as I watched Max stick a new note in that column.

"Let's sit down and drink that coffee before it gets cold," he said leading me to the sofa. "I'll tell you all about what I found."

"For a small town, their records are well kept and much of them are digital but they haven't all been converted yet. I had to dig through some dusty old records to find a list of previous owners of the castle and to see if I could find the original records of when it was built, possibly find some building plans." Max winced as he took a sip of coffee. He reached for the carafe to pour some hot coffee into his cup to warm it. He motioned with the carafe, "Need a warm up?"

"Sure," I said and held my cup out. Max seemed to be taking a long time in telling the story of what he found. I wondered if Finn was rubbing off on him. Maybe he would develop an Irish brogue too. I smiled at the thought.

Max sat back and continued. "I finally came across the original plans for the castle. It was built in the 1850s and passed down through the Muir family. I found a diagram, or a building plan of sorts from back then and took a picture of it." Max put down his coffee and woke his laptop. With a few clicks, he brought up the picture of the diagram. He split his screen and next to it he opened the picture he'd taken of the diagram found with James. We both leaned forward and studied it.

"Look at the similarities," Max said as he pointed from one to the other. "The only difference is that this area in the original is now labeled dovecote in the drawing James had." He pointed to James' diagram." He sipped some more coffee. "And that's only the beginning."

I sat back. Only the beginning?

"I traced the owners of the castle and then the lodge when it was built in 1898. Sir Sean Muir, the owner and the person Finn said was friends with Shackleton, was the one who built the lodge. I guess he preferred more modern accommodations." Max smiled. "Muir had no children, so the property passed to a cousin in America when he died in 1955. The cousin apparently had no interest in a castle in Ireland that had begun to deteriorate during the Great Depression but rather in the money generated by selling it and the lodge. After 1955 it passed through a couple of owners but then, more important to us, it was purchased in 2005 by Peter Callahan."

I didn't realize I'd been holding my breath. I let it out slowly as the connection began to form in my mind.

"And there's more," Max said draining his coffee cup. He set his cup down and picked up his laptop again. "I was able to download some digital copies of newspaper articles that documented his arrival in Dingle and eventually his murder."

"Murder?" I watched as Max pulled up the documents with the articles. "Was that the murder in the lodge that Millie talked about?"

Max turned his laptop toward me so I could begin reading. "The very same."

I began reading the first article.

Our town is pleased to welcome the new owner and resident of Castle Glas and Lodge, Peter Callahan, PhD. Dr. Callahan distinguished himself as a scholar of Irish history and folklore and is a friend and colleague of our very own Daniel Mahone who went off to teach in America. He has retired from his teaching and researching position at the College of William and Mary in Williamsburg, Virginia. It has always been a dream of his to own a castle and he looks forward to exploring whatever secrets of Irish history the Castle Glas may reveal to him. Secrets or not, Dr. Callahan says he will enjoy the rich countryside and the wonderful fresh sea air that our town of Dingle has to offer.

I scrolled a bit farther down the page to reveal the picture that accompanied the article. It was black and white but featured a very fine looking man in his sixties who had a pleasant smile that crinkled his eyes a bit. A full head of hair was spackled with gray and he had a bit of a beard that graced his chin.

"A very distinguished looking man." I sat back. "So Daniel Mahone has a Dingle connection as well. I wonder if he's still around?" I looked at Max who shook his head.

"Daniel Mahone died in a motorcycle accident a few months before Callahan's murder. His wife stayed in the States since their children were there but his body was sent home here for burial. It was a last wish."

Max wiggled his mouse around and clicked to bring up another article. This one was about an archeological dig at the castle. It explained that Peter Callahan wanted to search the grounds to see if any artifacts of previous owners might still be buried on the grounds and if so, what they might lend to the understanding of the history of the early days of the castle. Nothing was discovered before the search had to be called off because of the castle walls being compromised. It was deemed too dangerous to continue. Callahan vowed to raise more money to shore up the walls so the exploration could continue.

I waved my hand at the article on the screen. "Obviously he didn't raise enough money before he was murdered."

"No," said Max as he brought up another article for me to read. "He was killed shortly after that article was written." He turned the laptop to me again. "Here's the first article that appeared after the murder."

Emergency personnel were called to the Castle Glas and Lodge at the request of May O'Leary, housekeeper for the owner of the castle and lodge, Dr. Peter Callahan. She found the body of Dr. Callahan on the floor of the library and thought he had taken a fall from the bookshelf ladder. When it was determined there was nothing they could do for Dr. Callahan, the coroner and the Garda were called to the lodge. Coroner Ferngal determined that a blow to the head had led to the death of Dr. Callahan but reserved judgement as to whether the fall caused it.

"Garda? What is the Garda?" I asked looking up at Max for a moment.

"Garda is the name for the police force here."

"Oh," I said remembering that I just referred to them as the police like I did back home. It was a reminder that I was in a foreign country, not home. I continued reading.

The housekeeper told the Garda that the library seemed to be in disarray, not the usual organization that Dr. Callahan kept. She was understandably upset and frightened. The investigation will continue and we will keep you informed of its progress.

There was a picture of the castle and lodge and the picture of Dr. Callahan again. "The library was in disarray, it says. Could that mean there was a fight or was someone looking for something?"

"Good question," Max said. He took his laptop, made a few clicks and brought up another article. "This might tell you a bit more."

The investigation continues into the death of Dr. Peter Callahan and the findings are unsettling. Coroner Ferngal has determined that the blow to the head which caused the death was not the result of a fall from the library ladder. Indeed, the coroner has concluded that the blow was caused by the heavy candlestick that was in the room. Upon examination, the candlestick was found to have traces of Dr. Callahan's blood on it. A forensic team examining the room that was reportedly in disarray, suspects it was from someone searching the room for something of value which means that Dr. Callahan could have been murdered during a robbery. The housekeeper told the garda that there had been a visitor earlier in the day but she didn't know when he'd left since she had been out for a bit doing chores in town.

My mind was racing. Whoever killed Callahan was apparently looking for something of value in the library. Thornbury seemed obsessed with the library when he first arrived, so much so that he went into town to look through the books we donated. Max was scrolling and clicking on his laptop again. I wasn't sure what he was looking for.

"Did anyone ever discover who the visitor was that the housekeeper mentioned?" I asked.

Max shook his head. "No, they were never able to trace him. According to this article, he pointed to the computer screen, the housekeeper told the garda he introduced himself as an associate of Callahan and she let him in. Callahan met with him in the library. She was in a hurry to go into town and didn't pay much attention to the visitor so her description was very vague."

"Is the housekeeper still around? I wonder if we talk with her and show her a picture of Thornbury, maybe she would recognize him?"

"Why would we do that?" asked Max his eyebrow raised again.

"I remember Thornbury saying something about having been here previously with a friend and he was familiar with the library. It seems only logical that his being here might be a piece of the puzzle we're looking for."

"That's my sleuth!" said Max and quickly added, "I mean, that's my sweet investigator." He grinned. "You really do have a nose for this."

"Are you saying I'm nosey now?" I frowned at him as though I was serious.

Max threw his hands up in surrender. "I'm just saying that you have a good eye for clues and a sharp mind that connects the dots. You, my dear, would make a wonderful partner in law enforcement."

"Okay," I said laughing at the preposterous idea, "but let's get back to that housekeeper. Is she still in Dingle?"

"I don't know but I can check around tomorrow. Maybe Finn or Millie knows."

A yawn caught me by surprise and I raised a hand to cover it. "All this mental exercising is tiring. Sorry."

He patted my knee and closed his laptop. "It's okay. I think we've given ourselves enough to think about for one night. I'll check on Callahan's housekeeper tomorrow but we still need to figure out what it is that sent James to the castle and why Thornbury seems to be so interested in it. I'm quite certain that the instrument you saw him putting batteries into was a metal detector and that's exactly what the person in the video from the trail camera had." He rose and held out a hand to help me up. "Keep your eyes on him and let me know if you find out anything more." Max wagged a finger at me. "But by all means, be careful. We don't know exactly who or what we may be dealing with."

I saluted him. "Yessir!"

Max grinned. "Okay then." He pulled me into his arms and tenderly kissed me. When the soft kiss was over, he held me by the shoulders and looked seriously into my eyes. "I mean it. Be careful. I don't want anything to happen to you."

I could feel my eyes glisten with tears. "That works two ways you know." I turned before I could make a fool of myself with the emotions that seemed to be surging through me. I chuckled to myself as I picked up our tray of empty coffee cups. What's going on? I'm not the one who's pregnant with hormones dancing through me. As I heard Max close the door behind me, my heart was doing another happy dance. I was going to be a grandma. Yes. But I was also feeling closer to Max than I ever had before.

19

It was a misty Wednesday morning. Left over raindrops from the overnight rain fell from the leaves. I hoped the sun would break through for the Kellys last morning with us. It would be nice for them to have a sunny drive to the airport in Shannon. Perhaps not all of their memories of Ireland would be bleak and depressing. I feared it would take quite a while before they ever had warm thoughts about their time here.

Linda asked Evelyn and me to join them for breakfast. Normally I would have been up to Thornbury's room to freshen it but I figured I could do it later. He would probably be going out somewhere after breakfast and I needed the extra time anyway to change his linens.

"Casey, I want you to know how grateful we are for the hospitality you and your daughter have shown us. You especially. You have shared our grief in a way that was comforting."

I could see Evelyn's smile broaden as she said, "Mom is very good at that. She knows first hand how the death of a loved one can be so difficult to handle, especially one that is so sudden." Evelyn looked at me and patted my hand that was fidgeting with the napkin in my lap. "She helped me so much when Dad died."

There was no way I could answer with the big lump in my throat. I took a sip of coffee and dabbed at my eyes with my napkin. When I finally thought I could talk, I said, "I wish you both a safe trip home and time to heal. The wound will leave scars but in time there will be healing. God will see you through and we'll be praying for you long after you leave."

The dining room was quiet for a few minutes. Patrick looked up from studying his plate of yet untouched food. In a whisper he said, "Thank you."

The sun began to penetrate the misty fog of the morning. There were lots of hugs at the door when the Kellys were ready to leave. At least they would have a nicer trip to the airport with the sunshine. We all stood at the front door under the portal and waved goodbye as they circled the drive and headed out. Charles and Finn went off in one direction to work outside on moving some large rocks to accent one of the garden areas and Max said something about going into town to the bakery to pick something up for Millie. He gave me a wink as if I should know what he meant but turned and strode toward the car before I could ask.

Inside, I took a deep breath to try to clear my head and think about what I needed to do next. The Kellys room would need to be cleaned and Thornbury's linens needed to be changed. I found Millie gathering the linens and things we would need for both rooms.

"Nary a peep out of Professor Thornbury this morning, eh?" Millie straightened with the load of linens in her arms.

"Thornbury?" I suddenly realized I hadn't seen him at breakfast. "Do you suppose he's sleeping in? Or did he sneak out without our notice?"

Millie shrugged. "Maybe we should leave his room until after lunch. I hate the thought of walkin' in on the man."

"Let's do the Kellys' room first and then decide what to do about Thornbury," I said with a nod. I grinned at her. "That's the plan and I'm stickin' to it."

Millie gave a hearty laugh. It was good to hear after all the sadness of the morning. I hoped the Kellys would have an uneventful trip home. Linda had promised to write and I promised I would keep in touch as well.

Linda left a note for Millie on the mirror saying how much she had appreciated all the wonderful food at breakfast and the lovely afternoon teas. I saw Millie bite her lower lip and swipe at a tear when she read it. The simple kindness meant a lot to her.

We thoroughly cleaned the Kellys' room so it would be ready for new guests that Evelyn told us would arrive next week. I smiled as I surveyed the room one more time before closing the door. It was comfy and cozy looking. I loved what my daughter had done with each room. Guests would surely appreciate every detail she put into it.

When we got to Thornbury's door, the Do Not Disturb tag was hanging from the doorknob. The sound of snoring crept through the door. I looked at Millie and shrugged then nodded at the room across the hall. "Let's put the linens in there until we need them," I whispered. "We'll have a morning break."

Down in the kitchen, I warmed a cup of coffee from the morning's pot while a new pot was brewing in case the men decided to come in for a cup. Millie fixed her tea or rather, she wet the tea as I had learned the Irish phrase went.

"What are we doing for afternoon tea?" I asked Millie. "Max said he was running an errand to the bakery."

"I'm thinkin' that was an excuse," said Millie with a smile. "He was askin' me questions about the housekeeper that was here when the murder happened and I told him she had decided to join her sister at the bakery instead of keepin' house any longer." She rested her chin on her hand and sighed. "I think the shock of finding the body and then discovering that it was murder was too much for her. She wanted nothing to do with housekeeping after that."

"So the Merry May Bakery is two sisters?"

"Aye. Merry and May O'Leary. The two never married and when their father died, he left them the bakery. At first May wanted nothing to do with it. She helped Merry but she didn't want to partner with her. That changed after the murder. She felt safer helping Merry out. They changed the name of the bakery to Merry May and they seem to be doing quite well together."

"Well, their goods are delicious."

We both looked up as Evelyn came into the kitchen laden with bags of groceries. Millie jumped up quickly and offered a hand. "You shouldn't be carryin' such a heavy load," Millie scolded.

"I didn't think I'd bought that much," Evelyn said with a chuckle. "And don't be scolding me Millie. I get enough of that from my mother." She turned to me and winked. "Besides, the doctor said I should just continue to do what I normally do as long as I feel good."

I was up to help put groceries away. "That's fine, Evelyn, but let us pamper you a bit. Heaven knows as that tummy of yours grows, you'll welcome the attention."

Evelyn put a hand to her middle. "I still can't believe it. It doesn't seem real."

"It will be real enough soon," said Millie. She looked at the parcels of meat and fish that Evelyn had bought. She held one up in each hand. "And look. You're all ready to eat for two."

Evelyn and I totally lost it. Coming from Millie, it sounded even funnier than it was. We were almost bent over laughing when Charles and Finn walked into the kitchen. "What's going on?" Charles asked. "Did we miss out on something?"

"Just a little female humor," I gasped as I tried to stop laughing. I swiped laugh tears from my face. "Are you fellows ready for a little coffee or tea? Millie and I just made some."

"Sure," said Finn. He looked as bewildered as Charles but neither questioned what we may have been laughing at. Smart men.

As Finn and Charles settled down with Evelyn for a morning break, a knock came on the kitchen door. Millie went to answer it and opened the door to find Thornbury on the other side looking a bit penitent.

"Madam, I know I missed breakfast time this morning but I was wondering if I might have a spot of tea and perhaps if there is anything leftover?" He left the question kind of hang in the air.

Millie looked at Evelyn who nodded. "Aye, Professor. Have a seat in the dining room and I'll see what I can find for you."

"Thank you," he said. "I'm so grateful."

Millie started the tea and I opened the refrigerator to find the plate of sliced cheeses and fruits that we'd set there from the morning. I added a croissant and a couple of rolls and then gathered a plate and silverware. The two of us took it into the dining room with the tea.

"I hope this will do, Professor," I said. "Will you be joining us for afternoon tea?"

"I will," he said with a nod reaching for some cheese. "I plan to work in the library here today if that won't inconvenience anyone?" He lifted his eyebrows as he asked.

"No, that will be fine," I said. "Millie and I need to change your linens today and replace your towels so that will work out for all of us."

"Excellent," said Thornbury and plopped a chunk of cheese into his mouth.

For a man who had slept in, he still looked a bit sleep deprived. There were dark circles beneath his eyes. I wondered if his research had kept him up late last night.

I volunteered to clean the breakfast dishes from Thornbury while Evelyn and Millie were off admiring the work Charles and Finn had done that morning in the gardens. Just as I put the last dish in the dishwasher, Max returned from town with the bakery for afternoon tea and a loaf of fresh baked cinnamon raisin bread. He pulled the bread from the bag and held it out to me. "May said we should enjoy it while it's at its freshest." He grinned.

"Toasted?" I said taking the loaf from him.

"Of course. I'll get the butter out." He opened the refrigerator and pulled out the butter dish. "And is that fresh coffee I smell?"

"Fresh enough," I said as I sliced two pieces of bread and plopped them into the toaster. "You are sharing the bread, right?"

"Of course." Max poured coffee for the two of us and sat down. "But only because May promised to bring another loaf when she comes tomorrow."

I spun around. "She's coming here? Tomorrow?"

He nodded. "Yes. It took some coaxing but her sister helped me to convince her. She hasn't been here since Callahan's murder and she's understandably frightened. Her sister convinced her that facing her fears would be healing."

I pulled the toast from the toaster and put a piece on each of two plates. It smelled so good. I sat down with Max. "So what's the plan here? Do we get her to identify Thornbury as Callahan's visitor? And what then? That doesn't prove he was the killer. It just proves he was probably the last to see the man alive."

"One step at a time," said Max wiping a dribble of butter from the corner of his mouth. I handed him a napkin from the holder on the table. "We'll see what she can tell us of that day and if we can get her a look at Thornbury, we'll see if she remembers him."

"That could be tricky," I said trying not to groan with pleasure at the scrumptious bite of cinnamon raisin bread I had in my mouth. "He's working in the library today but who knows if he'll be around tomorrow." I picked a raisin out and plopped it into my mouth. "The man looked awfully tired when he finally got out of bed this morning. He missed breakfast and we fixed him a plate when he came begging at the kitchen door. If I thought he was the type, I'd say he'd been out partying all night."

Max held his piece of toast up but stopped before taking a bite. He looked at me strangely and then finished off his cinnamon raisin bread in a couple of bites. He brushed crumbs from his hands, rose quickly and kissed me on the cheek. "Thanks for the toast. I'll be back." Before I could answer, he was out the door. What got into him?

I savored my last bite of toast and finished just in time to see Millie and Evelyn come in. "There's some fresh baked cinnamon raisin bread Max is willing to share if you'd like a piece. It's wonderful." I saw Evelyn head to the counter immediately. It was one of her favorites. "I'll get started in Thornbury's room. Millie you can join me when you're ready."

"Thanks," Millie said to Evelyn who asked if she wanted her bread toasted. "I'll be there in a quick wink to help," she said to me.

The towels and cleaning supplies were already in the room across from Thornbury's so I didn't need to get anything from the storage room. I tiptoed across the gathering room to take a quick look into the library to be sure Thornbury was true to his word and would be in there. He was. I saw him shuffle through books on the shelf again like he had done before. Always searching it seemed but never finding what he wanted. What did he want? I backed away and went up the stairs to start on his room.

I began in his bathroom. All the towels were heaped in a pile on the floor. It looked as though he'd used every one we'd placed in there and they were more than just damp. Some were soiled with what looked like mud. What in the world was he doing? Where had he found all the mud? Then I remembered that it had rained the night before. He must have been caught in it. Foolish man.

Just as I finished the bathroom, Millie came in and started stripping the bed linens. I began running a duster over things. Most of his books and papers were put away, I assumed, in his case. The armoire door was ajar and I opened it a bit more to peer inside. The black clothes we'd seen strewn in his room before were now hung inside but they looked wet. I touched the shirt. Damp. So I was right. He had been caught in the rain. On the floor of the armoire sat a pair of boots that still sported streaks of mud as if someone had tried to wipe them clean but failed.

"Our professor appears to have been caught in the rain," I said to Millie. She came over and peered at what I had seen. She nodded her head.

"Aye, and the mud," she said pointing to the boots.

"The towels are muddy. He must have tried to clean the boots off. I'm surprised we didn't see any mud on the floor downstairs."

"Maybe he carried them up to the room."

I nodded. That made sense. I closed the door and turned to help Millie make the bed. As we tucked the top sheet in, Millie asked, "So Max was excited about something. Do you know what excited him?" She reached for the quilt and tossed it on the bed. "He was in a hurry to have Charles and Finn to go with him to the castle."

"I don't know. That man doesn't always tell me everything he's about." I pulled on a corner of the quilt as the two of us smoothed it out over the bed. "I'm sure he'll tell us when he's ready."

We finished the room in time to fix lunch. Before the men came in the back door they took their boots off explaining that they were muddy. Max handed me a muddy camera and asked me to wrap it in a towel. Was this the trail camera? What happened? They must have dropped it in a mud puddle. I grabbed an old towel we used as a rag and wrapped the camera so it wouldn't drop bits of dirt and mud on the floors. The guys banged their boots against the back step to shake the mud off. Charles called out for the brush that was stored under the small bench in the entry so they could remove the muddy clumps that were stubbornly clinging to the boots. I set the camera down and gave him the brush, then went to fetch a couple of wet rags. At least they wouldn't be using their bath towels.

When they were done, they left the boots out in the sun to dry and padded to the sink in their stockinged feet to wash their hands. As they sat down to their bowls of cabbage soup and rolls Max said, "As soon as we're done eating, I want to look at that disk from the trail camera." Charles nodded.

"What's on the disk?" I asked as Millie and I sat down with our soup.

"We don't know for sure," said Charles, "but someone took the time to splash a bunch of mud on the camera to cover the lens." So that explained it.

"I'm hoping that the camera caught the culprit before he was successful." Max spooned soup into this mouth so fast I couldn't imagine he even knew what he was eating.

Finn excused himself as soon as he was done with his soup. "I need to repair those shamrocks before they dry out too much. Let me know what you find."

"What happened to the shamrocks?" I asked, a wave of anxiety passing over me. I was partial to those plants since I had suggested them and even helped plant them.

Finn shook his head. "Don't know exactly. Something got into them. Maybe an animal diggin' for some grub or someone trampling through them. They'll be okay if I get them upright again and cover their feet." He gave me a reassuring smile and was off.

Evelyn asked me if I needed Millie for anything this afternoon. I couldn't see where I would so Evelyn told her to go home early. We only had Thornbury for afternoon tea and judging from the fact that he hadn't left the library to go get lunch, he would probably be hungry and definitely show for it. But since there was only one for tea, she wouldn't need Millie. Evelyn started on the tea sandwiches and I went with my cleaning basket into the gathering room to dust and satisfy my niggling curiosity with a check on Thornbury.

I dusted around the gathering room but held off running the vacuum. If Thornbury truly was buried in research, I didn't want the noise to disturb him. It was strange though that he had closed the door to the library. Well, almost closed. The door needed a little adjustment. It wouldn't close all the way so there was a small opening that I could peer through to see into the library.

If Thornbury was doing research it was strange research. He was up the library ladder with a pile of books in one hand and the other hand feeling around the shelf and the back wall where he had removed the books. He replaced the books and leaned to the other side, removing more books and performing the same searching movements. That cinched it like a grand slam by the home team in the last half of the ninth inning. He was looking for. . .I saw it clear as day! The letters!

I figured the dining room could wait my dusting. It was cleaned after breakfast and I was sure it would look just fine. I put away my supplies and headed to my room for a little reading. There had to be something important in those letters. At least these would hopefully be in English unlike the letters I found from Costa Rica about orchids when my former boss was murdered.

20

My heart raced. The letters! Where were they? The last thing I remembered was putting them on my nightstand. They were gone! Did someone take them? Calm yourself, Casey. I took a deep breath. Think, I told myself, think. No one would have come into your room uninvited. Or would they? Had I left my door unlocked? Yes, many times. I was far enough removed from any guest rooms that I didn't worry about that. But who would know that I had the letters? I told no one. Not even Millie or Evelyn. I hadn't even told Max yet. We never got around to that at our brainstorming session. So, where were they?

I checked the drawer to the nightstand. It held my Bible and reading glasses for when my eyes were tired and also some hand lotion that I rubbed on each night because my hands got dry from all the cleaning solutions I used. I closed the drawer. As I did, my eye caught something on the floor in the slight space between the nightstand and the bed. I got down on my hands and knees and wiggled one hand into the space. Sure enough, it was the packet of letters. Sometime in the night, they managed to fall after I had placed them on the nightstand.

I grunted as I stood. Was I getting that old? Well, I was going to be a grandma. I smiled. A young grandma, I told myself.

The letters had lost their original rubber band when they fell from their hiding spot in the library but I had replaced it with a ribbon. I untied the bow and started with the letter on top. It was dated June 20, 1914.

My Friend,

I have taken refuge at my cousin's country estate in Kerry County. The relentless pursuit of those who would destroy me has taken its toll. The countryside is lovely and offers the peace that I seek. Castle Glas is an intriguing structure and though my cousin doesn't find it so comforting anymore, I enjoy walking the grounds and imagining all that may have taken place here.

My cousin still houses pigeons in the dovecote but his interest in them is waning as well. I find them friendly enough and enjoy saving bits of bread to feed them.

But I digress. You ask if you may have a word with me to explain yourself. I welcome an explanation. I have been accused of much, some without merit. Somehow we must put these rumors and falsehoods to rest. I welcome any possibility of doing so.

Yours,
Arthur

Arthur? That name sounded familiar. I reached to the coffee table where *The Case Of The Crown Jewels* lay. Opening it to the table of contents it only took a quick glance to see the name, Sir Arthur Vicars. He was the keeper of the keys to the safe that held the jewels when they were stolen. But who was the friend he was addressing in the letter?

I unfolded the next letter that was dated several weeks earlier and read.

Sir Arthur, my friend,

It is with deep regret that I find you so embroiled in the theft that unfortunately occurred under your watch. It is to some extent the reason I have chosen to travel as anonymously as possible to deflect the implications of your involvement.

My greatest desire is to meet with you and explain myself as best I can. I hope this letter will reach you. I understand that you have retreated to Kerry County.

If a meeting is agreeable to you, please give notice to the friend of mine who will call on you and will forward the information to me.

Your servant,
Francis Shackleton

Shackleton and Vicars. The two were the main suspects in the theft of the crown jewels and here they were corresponding after the fact. Had they actually met here? I started looking through the other letters but it was too confusing. I needed to get them organized. I unfolded each one and looked at the dates. Once they were all in order, I began reading through them. It seems there was a meeting of the two. The rumor that Shackleton was here at the castle was true but he was here to meet with Vicars, not as a friend of Sir Muir who owned the castle. The two continued to correspond after Shackleton had left. The last letter was the one that was most cryptic and yet most telling.

My dear Sir Arthur,

I fear that things have gotten most dangerous and I will need to rely upon you once again for help. Our meeting was most profitable and I was looking forward to seeing you once again. The Castle Glas is a wonderful place and I agree that the dovecote houses the lovely treasures that we so enjoy. Pigeons can be jewels of the air.

If you should sell off any of the precious pigeons you have kept so lovingly, I would appreciate your forwarding of a small share to our mutual friend who will see that I receive it. Perhaps the help will afford me opportunity to visit my brother.

Your consideration of me would be greatly appreciated.

Your grateful servant,
Francis Shackleton

Pigeons were jewels of the air? The dovecote housed the pigeons and were treasures? Just how much did a pigeon sell for that would help Shackleton out of a bind? And I wondered who the mutual friend was?

I looked at my watch. It was almost time for tea and I hadn't offered any help to Evelyn. I gathered the letters together and tucked them into the drawer underneath my Bible. If nothing else, they were a bit of history that I was sure those who collected such things would consider very valuable. The letters could actually be gems of a different sort. A real treasure.

As predicted, Thornbury showed up for afternoon tea. I asked him if his research was going well and I got a shrug and a grunt in response. I left him to his sandwiches and tea. Max was in the kitchen waiting on another piece of cinnamon raisin bread to toast.

"I have some things to share with you after dinner tonight," I said.

He raised an eyebrow. "Well, there is something of interest to share with you as well. Plus we need to decide how we will proceed tomorrow when May O'Leary comes. Are you up for a little plotting?" He gave me a questioning look.

"A little plotting, huh?" I sliced myself a piece of cinnamon raisin bread. "That depends upon how devious I have to be. I'm not so sure I'm all that good at it."

"Not a lot of planning," Max said slathering butter on his warm toast. "We just need to figure out how to get May and Thornbury close enough for May to get a good look at him.

"Hmmm," I said as mysteriously as I could. I tapped a finger to my chin. "I may just have an idea."

Max chuckled and took a big bite of his toast. He walked out nodding his head. I wasn't sure if it was because of enjoying the taste of the toast or my having an idea. I'd find out tonight.

I could see the excitement in Evelyn's face as we ate dinner and she told us about the free day together that she and Charles had planned. Evelyn was packing a picnic lunch and the two were going to the Great Blasket Island which was a forty minute ferry ride from the Dingle marina. Evelyn said it would be good to experience it first hand before recommending it to any guests.

"Honey, this was supposed to be a day away from work," I said forking a piece of her now famous lamb stew into my mouth. Even the leftovers were good.

"It isn't like I'm sitting at a computer or Charles is hammering away at something," Evelyn answered. "We'll just be like normal tourists only we'll also have the experience to offer to any guests looking for something to do."

Charles patted my arm. "It's okay." He looked to Evelyn. "I'll make sure she doesn't spend the day worrying about the Bed & Breakfast business."

I grinned broadly. Oh, if he only knew the real business Evelyn was about. He was going to learn what most of us already knew. He was going to be a daddy.

Max and I set a couple of cookies on a plate with some cups and a carafe of coffee. "We're off to put our heads together with this mystery of ours," I said as we left Charles and Evelyn with their coffees and dessert. Charles shot a wink at Max. Maybe there was something he knew that I didn't.

We met in Max's room again since that was where all the sticky notes were that displayed all the information we had gathered. I ducked out for a minute to retrieve the letters from my room and returned to find Max tacking up several more notes to the wall.

"What is the new information?" I asked as I set the letters down and poured myself a cup of coffee. I plopped one of the little chocolate brownie gems Evelyn had baked this afternoon into my mouth and stood beside him as we both studied the wall.

He pointed to a new sticky note under the Thornbury column that said muddied camera lens. I almost choked on my sip of coffee. After I gained control, I said, "Well, that explains all the mud in his room this morning. He tried to clean his boots off with the towels. What a mess."

Max shook his head. "Not a very smart man," he said. "You would think he'd realize we would find him out. His face was staring up at the lens as he dabbed mud over it."

I saw that Max had started a column for May O'Leary. I moved closer and squinted a bit to try to figure out what he'd written. "You'll have to help me." I stepped back shaking my head. "I can't figure out your shorthand."

"Basic information. She was the housekeeper when Callahan was killed. She knew he had a visitor and might be able to identify him. And her sister said she remembered a young man coming into the bakery to buy a few sandwiches and mentioned that he was going on a treasure hunt. Merry said May was very upset to learn the young man, who I suspect was James Kelly, would be going to the castle."

"They didn't try to stop him? Didn't they warn him it was dangerous?"

"Merry said they tried to warn him but he didn't look like he could be put off of his mission." Max poured another cup of coffee for himself and motioned to me with the carafe.

"No thanks," I said. "I know my limit."

"So between the story he told the O'Learys and the diagram of the castle in his possession, it's pretty obvious he was looking for something specific and most likely in the dovecote."

I smiled slyly at Max. "I think I may have a little more to add to that." I motioned him to the sofa. "Let's sit down and I'll show you." I held up the letters I'd set on the coffee tray and explained who had written them. "I found these while I was dusting off the top shelf in the library. I put them on my nightstand but I forgot about them when they fell between the nightstand and the bed. I found them again, fished them out and read them this afternoon. I think they might be what Thornbury keeps searching the library for."

"What did you find in the letters?" Max raised that eyebrow of his when he asked. He paged through the letters but didn't read them as he waited for me to tell him what I'd found.

I gave him the summary. "Sir Arthur Vicars and Francis Shackleton were the two main suspects in the theft of the crown jewels. Sir Arthur was staying here at the castle with his cousin Sir Sean Muir and said he was being pursued by others. Shackleton wanted to set up a meeting with Sir Arthur and work something out. The meeting apparently took place because the later letters indicate that. There's one in particular though that I think will interest you." I picked out the letter that spoke of the dovecote and handed it to him.

Max read through it frowning as he tried to decipher the words written in a fanciful handwriting. Then he jumped up and went to the wall of notes. He made a few notations and then held them stuck to his fingers until he could decide where they belonged. He put one in the column with notes about the castle and the other in the Thornbury column.

"If you think the letters are what he is searching for, then he must have seen them once before or at least known of their existence." Max was rubbing his chin and staring at the wall as if the answer would appear. Finally he turned to me. "Could Thornbury have been here to see Callahan and Callahan showed him the letters? Or maybe Callahan told him about the letters?"

"Some wise investigator told me once to search the facts in hand, not presuppose evidence not there." I smiled at him.

"You mean some wise guy," he said with a chuckle. Max turned back to the wall. "Okay my sharp little sleuth, let's both go over this." He began to point out the facts we had that connected the people on the wall. "Vicars and Shackleton were primary suspects in the jewel theft. Evidence shows they were both together at the castle at some time. The book, *The Case Of The Crown Jewels,* was written by a former local who knew Callahan well enough to have him write the foreword. Callahan wanted to retire to a castle in Ireland and picked this one. Callahan was an expert on Irish history and folklore. Thornbury claims to be an expert in the same field. Thornbury has a manuscript written by Callahan about the Irish crown jewels. James Kelly attended a seminar by Thornbury just before he came here searching for treasure. Thornbury's seminar followed the outline of the book. James had a diagram of the castle that showed the dovecote mentioned in the exchange of letters between Vicars and Shackleton that seemed to indicate there was treasure there." He looked sideways at me. "I don't believe for a minute that the treasure was the flock of pigeons Muir kept."

"So where does that leave us?" I felt like we'd just gone around in a big circle that hadn't accomplished anything.

"That leaves us with May O'Leary. If she can connect Thornbury to Callahan on the day he was murdered, we may have some motive. Callahan had information that Thornbury wanted about the jewels."

"But if he killed Callahan, he obviously did it before he got the information. Otherwise he wouldn't be searching the library or the castle grounds."

Max ran a hand back and forth over the top of his head. "We need to be sure May gets a good look at Thornbury."

"When is she coming?"

"Mid-morning. She said the baking will be done by then and Merry could handle the customers for a time."

"Okay, by then Thornbury should be done with his breakfast. I'll be sure to draw it out a bit by not having the tea water hot and whatever else I can think of."

"I'm sure you'll figure it out," Max said putting an arm around me and squeezing. "Now I guess we'd better call it a night. Big day tomorrow for all of us." He paused and grinned at me. "G'night Grandma."

I blushed. Grandma. Tomorrow Charles would know and I'd be able to tell the world. I gathered the dishes and cups and floated to the kitchen to set them in the dishwasher for the morning. I looked around at the things set out ready for breakfast and realized I would have to let Millie in on why I would be bungling the usual preparations for breakfast. I was sure she would play along. There seemed to be a bit of a sleuth in her too.

21

The morning dawned bright and sunny. There were butterflies in my stomach. Between the excitement of knowing Evelyn would tell Charles today they were expecting a baby and arranging for May to see Thornbury, I was more than a bit unsettled. I looked in the mirror one more time to be sure I had taken care of my hair and clothing. Yup, everything on and hair brushed. I took a deep breath and turned to go. There was a knock on my door.

"Mom?" I opened the door to Evelyn who looked a little pale. "Oh thank goodness you haven't gone to the kitchen yet. I need to talk to you."

I closed the door behind her as she came in and began to pace. "What's wrong? Are you feeling okay?"

"Right now I am," she said putting a hand to her forehead and holding it. "What was I thinking? We can't go on a boat ride. With my morning sickness I'm sure to lose my breakfast."

"I'm sure you'll be fine. The boat ride isn't that long and the worst that can happen is you feed the fish over the side." I smiled at her. "You won't be the first to do that and you can always claim seasickness."

Evelyn looked at me and frowned. "Seasickness? Come on Mom. After three years on a ship, Charles would find that excuse feeble."

"Honey, it's a much smaller boat. Besides, I think there's a few things in the kitchen that will help you out." I took her by the arm and led her to the door. "Come with me. I'll show you."

In the kitchen I found a box of saltine crackers and a bag of ginger cookies that we used for afternoon tea." I turned and handed them to her. "Try the crackers first. They always used to work for me."

"Of course," Evelyn said with a sigh. "I should have thought of that. It's the same thing we always told our passengers to eat when they turned green." She kissed my cheek and went to the counter to pull out a little plastic container to put a few crackers and cookies in. "I'll tuck these in my backpack with our sandwiches. Charles is going to carry our water and tea in his."

"You're going to have a beautiful day. Don't fret so much. What time do you leave?" I looked at my watch.

"As soon as Charles is ready. We had breakfast and so far I'm good. Maybe I'm getting past this phase." She crossed her fingers and held them up. "He told Finn to take the day off so it will only be Millie coming today."

"Okay." I clapped my hands together. "Let me get started on breakfast then for Max and me and I'll be ready to help Millie with the B&B breakfast for Thornbury. "Has he told you how much longer he's staying?" I avoided telling Evelyn our plans for Thornbury. She had enough to worry about today and I didn't want to spoil her time with Charles.

"He implied he was leaving this morning," Evelyn said as she tucked the crackers into her backpack that rested on a chair. "Said he'd done everything he could here. Whatever that was supposed to mean."

"Likes being cryptic, I guess," I rinsed the fry pan from Charles' breakfast eggs and prepared to fix some for Max. My hands shook a bit. If Thornbury planned to leave this morning, it might be a little more difficult to get him to stay long enough to meet with May.

Evelyn hoisted the backpack over her shoulders. "If Thornbury does leave, you can always do his room tomorrow. Let Millie go home after breakfast. That way we can all get the day off. Maybe you and Max can find something exciting to do together as well."

I cupped her face in my hands. "You've got this, kiddo. It's going to be a special day. I just know it." I brushed a stray hair behind her ear. "Now get out of here."

Evelyn laughed. "Yes, ma'am!"

Max came in just as I was about to turn his eggs. "Oh good," I said waving the spatula in the air. "I was afraid I was going to have to eat these." I flipped the eggs and reached for the toast that had just popped up. I set the eggs on the plate next to his toast and took them to the table. "There you go. Eggs over easy and toast. Can I get you anything else?"

"Answers. Any answers you can," Max said as he reached for the coffee carafe. "I had a hard time falling asleep last night. That wall of questions kept staring at me."

"Did you try turning the light off?" I said with a little chuckle as I attempted to lighten his mood.

He gave me a look that said "Do you think I'm stupid?" I sat down with my cereal and decided to let him eat in peace. When he had soaked up the last of the egg yolk using his toast, he sat back in his chair with his coffee cup in hand. "Are you okay with all of this today?"

I shrugged and set down my cup. "Sure." I shrugged again. "A little nervous but I'll be okay."

He smiled broadly. "I have every confidence in the world that you can handle this." He rose just as Millie came into the kitchen. "I have to go run an errand and pick up our guest. I promised her a ride to the lodge."

"A guest?" Millie asked as she hung her jacket on a peg by the kitchen door. "Do we have a new guest?"

I looked at Max. "I'll explain it to her," I said. He nodded and left. "Sit down a minute, Millie. I have to tell you about a couple of things I need your help with this morning."

"Ah, but we must get the porridge started and the tea water heated."

"It can wait a few minutes," I said waving her to a kitchen chair to sit down. "That's part of what I need to talk with you about."

Millie looked totally confused as I tried to explain that we needed to be slow with breakfast this morning so that Thornbury would not leave too soon. I told her that he was planning to check out this morning and be on his way but we needed to prevent that before May O'Leary arrived.

"May?" Millie shook her head. "I'm thinkin' she won't be coming here. She doesn't want to see this place again. That's why she won't deliver any baked goods here."

"Max has convinced her that she will feel much better if she faces her fears and comes to the lodge. He's promised her that it will help her overcome the bad memories and her sister agreed. That's who he went to fetch." I covered her hand with mine. "Millie, we think Thornbury was the visitor that May saw here before Peter Callahan was murdered."

Millie pulled her hand away and put it to her mouth. "No!" She looked at the door to the dining room and whispered, "Thornbury? Here? On that day?"

I lowered my voice. It was probably safer since he could be lurking if he were up earlier than usual. "Yes. Max and I have a lot of clues that seem to point to Thornbury being here and we need to have May identify him as the visitor. Will you help me?"

She looked worried. "Of course but be careful, Casey." She lowered her voice even more. "He could be the killer."

I nodded slowly. "I know. It's possible but we don't know that for sure." I rose and held a finger up. "One step at a time."

Millie and I took our time putting out the usual breads and rolls on the sideboard. Thornbury came into the dining room as I set the plate of rolls down and went straight to the kettle that usually held the hot water for tea. He picked it up, frowned and then wiggled it at me. "It appears the water is gone."

I took it from his hand. "I'm sorry Professor Thornbury," I said as sweetly as possible. "We're running a bit behind this morning. Millie was a little late in getting here. It's been a bit of a confusing morning." I started for the door to the kitchen but turned. "Oh, Evelyn mentioned you might be leaving us this morning?"

"Yes," he said as he placed several rolls on his plate. "Is there no cheese and fruit?"

"Sorry," I said. I turned to the door again. "I'll be right back with the cheese and fruit tray."

In the kitchen, I said quietly to Millie, "I think we've already stretched his patience a bit. Let me take the cheese and fruit in. Fill the kettle for tea water but I'll get that later."

Millie nodded but gave me a worried look. "Don't let his temper boil over."

I smiled. "Not planning on it."

Instead of setting the tray on the sideboard, I set it in front of Thornbury who had poured himself a glass of juice. He was buttering a roll and didn't bother to look up at me. "Is the water for tea available yet?" he asked taking a bite of his roll. "And need I order my porridge again?"

"Porridge? I'll make sure Millie has started it." I walked slowly to the door as if in thought. "Oh, and I'll check on that water for tea."

In the kitchen again, I let out the breath I found myself holding. "I don't know how much longer we can delay. I'm texting Max to see how he's doing." I picked my phone out of my pocket and plucked out a text.

Any ETA?

I put my phone back in my pocket when I didn't get an immediate response and picked up the tea kettle to take to the dining room. "I'll be back in a minute for the porridge. Perhaps if I keep him talking it'll take a while for him to eat it." I backed through the door to the dining room and almost ran into Thornbury. Was he listening at the door?

"This won't take but a moment to heat and then I'll wet your tea for you if you like," I said.

"Wet my tea?" He picked up a couple of tea bags and plopped them into a teapot.

"Yes. Pour the water into the teapot to let the tea seep?" Did he not know the phrase that Millie used all the time? If he were such an expert on Irish history, an Irishman himself, I would have thought he'd be familiar with the phrase.

"Of course, yes." He sat back down with another roll and waited for me to bring the teapot to him. I set it down carefully next to his teacup.

"I'll be right back with your porridge," I said. As I passed through the kitchen door, my pocket vibrated. I pulled out my phone and read the message. Millie stood anxiously watching me. "Max says forty-five minutes should do it." I looked up at her. "I think we're good." Millie nodded at me and handed me the bowl of porridge. I noticed a slight tremor in her hands. "It's fine, Millie. We did just fine."

I took the porridge in and placed it in front of Thornbury who grunted a thank you. He was truly upset with the delays. I put a tea bag into another teapot and poured hot water in. Taking an extra cup from the sideboard, I sat in the chair opposite Thornbury. "I hope you don't mind if I join you. I could use a spot of tea before I start my morning chores."

Just for something to do with my hands, I dunked my tea bag up and down willing it to hurry up and give me something to drink. My mouth felt dry. Thornbury was wolfing down his porridge despite the fact I'd brought it to him piping hot. I tried to think of something to ask so he would have to answer and slow his eating. I settled on, "I understand your research is finished? I hope you found what you were looking for."

He grunted but stopped with his spoon halfway to his mouth. "Hardly. You people have ravaged the library. The books I counted on being there were not and the town library gave me little access to what they had." He shoveled the spoonful of porridge into his mouth.

"What books were you looking for? Perhaps I have them in my room." I poured a cup of tea from my tea pot that had finally yielded a tea that was drinkable.

Thornbury put his spoon in his bowl of porridge and clasped his hands together above it. "And what books, my dear lady, would you have interest in that you took them to your room?"

I stirred a bit of sugar into my tea. His tone was so condescending I found it insulting. "When I first came, I was interested in learning more about the castle and its history. I found several books that caught my eye. One was a collection of pictures and history of castles in Ireland." I took a sip of tea trying to draw out the time as I glimpsed at my watch. "Unfortunately the pages that held information about Castle Glas, the name of the castle before the new owners changed it, were gone from the book." His eyes flickered slightly. "And then I happened upon a book I found very interesting." I took another sip of tea and slowly set the cup back down. I could tell he was losing patience. His eyes had narrowed and he frowned. "It was very informative about a legend that involved the castle. I believe the title is *The Case Of The Crown Jewels*."

He stared at me for a moment and seemed to be processing the information to decide what to do with it. He picked up his spoon again and dug around his porridge as if the answer was in the bowl. Finally he said, "And did you learn anything?" He stared at me again.

"Oh yes," I said lightly, "there was quite a bit to learn. It was all about the theft of the Irish crown jewels and how the castle may have been involved." Another sip of tea and I glanced again at my watch. It was just about time to move him to the library as we had planned.

He looked up for a moment and then dug into his porridge again. "I've read that book. It makes no mention of Castle Glas only that Sir Arthur Vicars may have stayed somewhere in Kerry County where he was shot by the IRA but that was long after the theft."

I had his attention. I could tell by the look on his face that he was suspicious and curious as to what I might know. I set my cup down. "Oh, well maybe I just assumed it was in the book because that's where I found a letter signed by Francis Shackleton to Sir Arthur and it talked about Sir Arthur's stay here with his cousin Sir Sean Muir." He straightened. Yes, I definitely had his attention.

"Letter? You found a letter?" The thought of the letter must have made him salivate. He brought the napkin to his mouth and wiped it.

“Yes, a letter.” I took another sip of tea only because I now had the upper hand and I was enjoying the aggravation it caused him. “Would you care to see it?”

“Yes, of course,” he said quickly. He rose as if he expected me to lead him to it. “It could be just what I need to finish my research.”

“If you’ll give me a minute, I’ll meet you in the library. I just need to take these things into Millie and I’ll fetch the letter.” He let out an impatient sigh. “Would you like to see the book as well?”

“No, thank you,” he said abruptly. “I’m well acquainted with the book.” He turned and left I assumed, in the direction of the library. I’ll just bet you’re well acquainted with the book, I thought. It’s your outline for your bogus seminars.

22

With Thornbury on his way to the library I allowed myself to take a deep breath and let it out slowly before I took a few dishes in to Millie. I explained to her that I was on my way to my room and then to the library. "When Max arrives with May, tell him that's where I am but don't mention Thornbury is there as well. Max will know that and we don't want May to know." Millie nodded. She looked very nervous but I had faith in her. She would pull it off.

In my room I picked up the one letter we had decided to let Thornbury look at and slipped it into the pocket of my apron. It was the one that spoke of the treasure and the dovecote in the castle. I checked my watch again. Five minutes give or take and Max should be here. He knew how important the timing was. If he was delayed, he would have texted me by now.

Thornbury was pacing the library when I went in. He stopped short when he saw me. I walked slowly forward and waved a hand about as I indicated the bookshelves. "What do you think of our renovation? We've tried to make it a little cleaner and safer for our guests. We didn't want them climbing too high on the ladder. It could be very dangerous, don't you think?"

Either the remark did not register or else his mind was so set on seeing the letter that he missed the implication entirely. "The letter, madam, the letter?" He held his hand out.

"Oh, of course," I fumbled in my pocket as if I didn't know where I'd put it. Where was Max? I couldn't hold this man much longer. And what if he knew there were other letters? What then? Would he demand I produce them? If the letters were what he was searching for then he would know there was more than one.

Suddenly I heard a growl. Where had Allie come from? She brushed up against my leg. "Sit, girl," I said hoping that for once she would obey. "Sit." I pushed her backside down and she sat but the hair on the back of her neck was still standing up.

Thornbury started forward and stopped when Allie's backside came up again and she bared her teeth. He stared at her as he said, "The letter, please."

I pushed Allie back down with another command to sit and plucked the letter from my pocket. "Ah, here it is." He snatched it from my hand as I held it out to him.

Thornbury unfolded the letter and walked to the open window where the light was better to read it. Open window? I didn't remember leaving a window open overnight. I was surprised Evelyn or Charles had neglected to check. Maybe Thornbury needed some air and opened it. I stroked Allie's ear. "Good girl."

He read through the letter and nodded his head. "Just as I thought," he mumbled to himself. "The dovecote." I watched as he read the letter again. He lifted his head and wrinkled his brow. "Is this all you found?" he asked as if accusing me of concealing more—which actually I was guilty of doing.

I started to answer but was interrupted by Max's voice. "The library is a bit different than you may remember it," he said as he ushered May O'Leary into the room. She started to look around then drew up short as she saw Thornbury standing by the window. I could hear her sharp intake of breath at the shock of seeing him.

There were a few moments of silence as Thornbury and May stared at each other. Finally Thornbury cleared his throat. "Miss O'Leary, we meet again." He nodded.

She looked frightened at first but seemed to gain a bit of confidence. "That we do, Professor Thornbury. That we do."

Max and I looked at each other. So, they knew each other but was he the visitor that day? Or did they know each other from another time? Maybe Thornbury knew her from the bakery. He'd been in town enough to have lunch. Perhaps he stopped in for sandwiches as James Kelly had.

"May, is this the visitor Peter Callahan had that day he was murdered?" Max asked without waiting another moment.

May seemed to hesitate. There was a look that passed between her and Thornbury but I couldn't tell what it meant. Finally she nodded. "Aye, that he is. The last one I remember from that day."

"Now wait a minute." Thornbury's accent seemed to have vanished suddenly. "What are you saying? You're not going to pin his murder on me. I was here after the fact."

"After the fact?" Max asked.

"After the fact." Thornbury folded the letter and put it in his pocket. "May here was standing over him. She claimed he fell from the ladder but he was too far away from it to have fallen."

"That's what you told me," May said her voice raised. "He tells me that Callahan was on the top rung and fell backward. He was standin' right there over him." She pointed to where I assumed Callahan's body had been.

While the back and forth between them was all very interesting, I didn't want to lose that letter that was now in Thornbury's pocket. I stepped forward with my hand out. "Professor, I'll have back that letter I showed you. It belongs to the lodge and its owners."

It only took a moment to realize my mistake. Thornbury grabbed my hand and in one quick motion he had me turned to face the others with my arm bent behind my back. I had no idea how he had produced a gun or from where, but it was there, pointed to my head. Allie lept forward with a ferocious growl but Thornbury managed to kick her before she could do any damage to him. She yelped and landed on her side. She had herself righted quickly and growling again at him. I was afraid she would attack again and cause Thornbury to shoot.

"Take it easy Thornbury," Max said as he quickly took hold of Allie's collar. She was still giving a low growl but had to be in some pain from the foot to her middle. He pulled her back a bit.

Thornbury pulled me away from them. "Back off!" He twisted my arm a bit making me wince. I refused to make a sound. He nodded at May. "I am not going to take the blame for a murder I didn't commit. It's all her fault. She killed Callahan because he wouldn't tell her where the jewels were."

"That's a lie!" May shouted at him. "There were no jewels here and you know it."

"You're wrong May," Thornbury said with a snarl. "The jewels were buried in the dovecote."

"That was before my father dug them up for Vicars. Peter Callahan knew that. He also knew that my father baked those jewels into a loaf of bread so that he could transport them to Shackleton. He just assumed my father had kept some for himself."

"Did he?" Thornbury snarled. "Isn't that how you and Merry put together such a nice bakery?"

Thornbury's grip seemed to loosen a bit as he

argued with May but the gun was still to my head. I wasn't moving.

"He did not!" May's face was red with anger. "I told Mr. Callahan that over and over again. My father wanted no part of those jewels. Shackleton was threatening him with some sort of political harassment which was the reason he helped him at all. But Mr. Callahan wouldn't believe me. He was ossified that day. The man was driven to drink by his quest to find those jewels. He came at me, hands at my throat, wantin' me to tell him where they were." She put a hand to her forehead. "Lord, forgive me, I was so scared. I felt the candlestick in my hand. I only wanted to make him let me go." Her voice began to falter. "I didn't mean. . ."

Max looked from May to Thornbury as he struggled to keep Allie from charging Thornbury again. "So you didn't kill him. But why don't you let Casey go before you hurt her?" He was looking at me and I could tell he was planning something. That Columbo look was in his eye.

"Oh no. I know how this works." Thornbury said nodding again to May. "She'll make me an accessory. I helped her move the body to the ladder to make it look like an accident. I'm not sticking around for the garda. He looked to May. "May, we can work this out if you'll show me the safe."

"Won't do no good," May said sniffling. "I still don't know the combination."

"No, but I do," said Thornbury easing his grip a little more. "I figured it out from his manuscript."

"The one you stole?" May asked.

"Borrowed, but yes. It was easy to figure out from his cryptic references."

May's mood seemed to lighten. What did she think was in the safe?

"The safe is behind the painting." She pointed to the one I had always admired as I dusted it. It was the one that looked like it was painted on glass and had been accented in gold.

"Too obvious," Thornbury said shaking his head in disgust. "I thought it was too obvious and I didn't look there. All of this could have been avoided if I'd found it sooner." He let go of my arm but kept a grip on my shoulder and the gun to my head. "May, if you'll help me we can both get out of this. I'll take you with me but I need your help."

"You're full of promises Tom, but you don't seem to be coming through on them."

Tom? May had called him Tom? I thought his first name was Edwin. This was getting more curious by the moment.

"I'll help you now but you had better not be acting the maggot again. This time I want my trip to America."

"All arranged." Thornbury was moving me toward the painting which hid the safe. "I have our passports and everything. If this safe holds what I think it does, we'll have plenty to get us there."

"Well, all right then," May said moving closer to us. "What is it you be needin'?"

Thornbury pushed me forward toward Max. I almost lost my balance but his free hand caught me. He pulled me close to him. "You okay?" I nodded as I rubbed my wrist where Thornbury had held it so tightly. We kept our eyes trained on the two in front of us who seemed to have plans we hadn't even begun to imagine in all our investigating.

Thornbury kept the gun trained on the two of us and Allie who was sitting but still emitting a low growl now and then. He pulled May over to him and transferred the gun to her hand. "Keep them in place." She had to hold it with two hands. I wasn't sure if it was because her hands shook slightly from nerves or if the gun was just too heavy for her to hold. Either way I hoped it wouldn't go off.

23

The painting came off the anchor pin with a lot of grunting and groaning on Thornbury's part. It had to be heavy. The frame alone was thick and made of some sort of plaster that was painted gold. I couldn't imagine the weight the glass painting added to it. I hoped he wouldn't drop it. It would be a shame to see it destroyed. I bit my lower lip as I watched him lower it to the floor and lean it against the bookshelf.

Sure enough, behind the painting was a wall safe, not terribly large but certainly big enough to hold jewels if that was what Thornbury was counting on. He spun the dial and pulled a small piece of paper from a pocket inside his jacket. He looked from the paper to the dial and twisted it back and forth until he was satisfied he had used the combination. A tug on the handle proved he hadn't. He swore. May's eyes flicked from us to Thornbury at that moment. I could feel Max tense as though he was ready to spring but he held steady as May quickly stared back at us again.

"It must go the other way," Thornbury mumbled. He spun the dial again and started over. This time it worked. "Success!"

May was distracted by his announcement and her head turned to look at Thornbury. At that moment, Max yelled at Allie, "Get him!" and let her go. As she jumped on Thornbury, Max tackled May who was too startled by the dog attacking Thornbury to know what hit her. The gun went sliding across the floor and thankfully stopped just before my feet. I picked it up quickly and pointed it at Thornbury.

"Allie! Down girl! Come!" I called to her hoping she would obey. I didn't want Thornbury to send her flying again with a kick. He was off balance and fighting to stay upright as she had hold of his pant leg and was shaking it fiercely.

The next moment there was a commotion behind me. I didn't want to turn and look for fear Thornbury would have at me if I was distracted. I heard a voice behind me say, "It's okay, Miss Casey. It's okay. We'll take it from here." A hand reached out and took the gun from mine. I looked around to see several of the garda with their guns drawn. Max had righted himself and put May back on her feet. Allie was still attached to Thornbury though. She was taking all of her frustration out on him.

"Allie! Come, girl! Come!" I didn't dare get close to Thornbury again. I didn't want him grabbing me a second time. I got down on one knee and patted the floor. "Come on girl, that's enough. Good girl. Good girl." She let go of Thornbury's leg and trotted over to me, obviously very proud of herself.

It only took a few minutes for the garda to arrest May and Thornbury for the murder of Callahan. They had heard enough from the door to figure it out. Max and I stood with Allie and watched. Max dropped his arm from around me and walked over to the safe. He turned to the man I had always called the police chief. I still had no idea what his official title was. "Do you mind if I have a look?"

"Let's have at it," the police chief said. "What could be so important in here?"

Max reached in and pulled out a letter and an old leather pouch that looked well worn. I looked over his shoulder as he unfolded the letter. I recognized the flowing handwriting. Max read the letter aloud.

My dear friend,

I have received the delicious loaf of bread you sent me through our mutual friend, the baker. He tells me he had to leave one ingredient out as the loaf was already too large. He will return it to you. I pray you will allow the precious treasures of the dovecote to keep guard over it.

I thank you again for your help in this matter. Your invaluable aid will be rewarded once I reach my destination.

Your friend and servant,
Francis

Max handed the letter to me and began to unfold the leather pouch. The inner pocket held a gold band. Was it a part of the crown jewels? There were no jewels in the pouch but I remembered that the list of crown jewels included several gold collars. I guess that's what this was, a necklace of sorts. It would have been difficult to bake it in a loaf of bread.

"Do you think it's part of the crown jewels?" I asked.

"Possibly," said the police chief. "We'll have to give it over to those who would know."

"You'll want the letters as well," I said. "They tell part of the story and I'm sure those who treasure the history, will want to keep them safe."

"You'll want this too," said Max walking over to the open window and taking down a small metal eyeball. He popped it open and took out the little disk inside. "If you have any trouble downloading it, let me know. I'm sure we can figure something out."

The police chief looked at the small disk in his hand. "Do you always come prepared to catch a murderer?"

Max laughed. He pointed a thumb at me. "You never know when Casey is going to find a dead body." They both had a good laugh at my expense and ignored my protests that it had been Allie who'd found the body. Allie raised her head from where she lay on the floor and thumped her tail. I had the feeling she was very pleased with herself.

Millie and Finn were in the gathering room waiting on us. Millie rushed forward. "Are you all right?"

I nodded my head. "Yes. We're both okay thanks to Allie's quick work on Thornbury." I patted our sweet pup's head again. "We need to keep an eye on her though. She took a good blow to the midsection from Thornbury. It probably wouldn't hurt to have her checked out at the vet."

"I can take her," Finn said. "Would be a pleasure." He smiled at Allie who lay down and rolled over for a belly rub. Finn obliged but carefully. He looked up at Max. "Sorry it took so long to get the garda here. It took a bit of convincing."

"You were right on time. Any sooner and they may have spooked our guests which might have gotten us hurt." Max reached over and put an arm around me again. "I was a little concerned about you."

"You were concerned?!" I tried raising an eyebrow like he always did but it didn't work. "I was the one with the gun to my head!" Millie paled. I made her sit down and I sat next to her. My knees had held me up thus far but I was beginning to feel the shock of all that had happened. "Thanks for your help, Millie."

"When Finn came with the garda and told me what was going on. . ." She searched me with her eyes as if making sure I was all in one piece and shook her head. Tears welled up and threatened to escape.

I gave Millie a hug. "It's okay. It all ended well." I sighed and leaned back. Chuckling I said, "I wonder how the day is going for Evelyn and Charles? I'm glad they missed all this excitement and I'm sure their excitement was a whole lot more fun."

Max smiled at me.

24

Our lunch turned into a late afternoon tea by the time the garda had taken Thornbury and May O'Leary into custody and gotten statements from Max and me. I didn't know about anyone else but I was famished. Millie, bless her heart, had spent time making up sandwiches while she waited for all the activity in the library and Thornbury's room to be done. We ate wonderful lamb sandwiches that Millie had set under the broiler to melt a bit of cheese on top. A little onion and some special sauce set it off perfectly.

Millie made lots of hot tea and even the coffee drinkers enjoyed the change of beverages. There was something a little more soothing about tea and our nerves began to settle down. Millie had sliced some of the cinnamon raisin bread for us as well. Max held a piece up and studied it a moment. "I'm glad she baked this before she knew what we were doing." We all laughed.

The garda had gathered all of Thornbury's things from his room. Among them they found a passport issued by the United States in the name of Tom Mahone. Mahone, I remembered, was the same last name of the man who wrote *The Case Of The Crown Jewels*, the book for which Callahan had written the foreword. I made sure the garda knew that because I was sure it all fit together.

As we were munching on cinnamon raisin bread and sipping some more tea when Max's phone buzzed. He excused himself and went into the kitchen to take the call. When he returned he was grinning. "Well, Millie, you were right. Thornbury, or Tom Mahone, certainly wasn't Irish but he did have an Irish connection in the form of a cousin from Ireland named Daniel."

"The one who wrote the book!" I put in quickly.

"Yes," Max said giving me his be-patient look. "Once the garda started questioning the two they have in hand, they began spilling everything probably hoping it would go easier on them. May was concerned that Merry might somehow be implicated by the fact that she was May's sister but it's apparent she knew nothing about what was going on between Thornbury and May."

"There was something going on?" I couldn't help myself. I had to ask.

"Yes. When Thornbury got all the information about the castle and its possible connection to the jewel theft, he made it his business to look May up. His cousin had told him the rumors that May's father, Seamus, may have been the mutual friend between Vicars and Shackleton. He pursued May relentlessly according to her.

When Callahan was murdered, Thornbury disappeared fearing he would be implicated or accused of the murder. There's still some question about who swung the fatal blow. Thornbury discarded his Tom Mahone name, gave himself credentials and set about giving the shady seminars about the crown jewels. He was actually wanted for fraud involving those seminars but they hadn't quite caught up to him. I think he was making one last attempt at retrieving what jewels might be at the castle and making a run back to the States.

There was some understanding that if May would help him, he would see that she made it to the

States and be able to start a whole new life for herself. She's not liked being stuck in the bakery."

"Oh dear," Millie said. "Imagine poor Merry. She must be so disappointed in her sister. Merry is such a sweet thing. I hope this doesn't reflect poorly upon her."

Finn patted Millie's hand. "She's well loved in this town. People will treat her fairly." He pulled his phone from his pocket. A text had just arrived. "Okay now. Dr. Kendall says to keep an eye on Allie and if she appears to be in any discomfort to bring her right in tonight. Otherwise he will see her tomorrow morning."

We all looked through the kitchen door that we had propped open so that Allie could be a part of our time together and yet still uphold the no-dogs-in-the-dining-room rule. She was happily gnawing on the bone from the lamb roast Millie had given her. If she had any discomfort, she wasn't showing it. She was in bone heaven.

"I still don't quite understand what James Kelly's part is in all this. Why was that poor boy digging up the castle grounds?" I poured myself another cup of tea and added a bit of sugar.

"Thornbury was questioned about that," Max said as he reached for a piece of chocolate brownie. "He denied any connection other than the fact that James had attended his seminar. He remembered a discussion about where jewels might be hidden in a castle and the subject of the dovecote being a perfect place came up. That probably explains Thornbury's searching as near to the place as he could as well. I don't know how he expected to dig—"

Max was interrupted by a raucous noise at the front door. We could hear bags being dropped on the floor followed by voices yelling, "We're home!! Where is everybody?"

"We're in the dining room!" I yelled back.

Charles came running in followed quickly by Evelyn. "I'm going to be a father!! For real! A father!" He looked like he was ready to dance around the table.

We all sat there calmly and grinned at him. Finally I rose and gave him a hug. "We know and we couldn't be more pleased."

Charles stepped back. "You know? How could you know? I just found out."

I laughed. "Well, Millie suspected long before any of us and Evelyn needed to tell me before she went to the doctor to confirm it and then Millie told Finn, and well. . ."

Finn's face turned red. "And I can't keep a secret. I told Max. I was too excited to keep it in."

Charles' look of bewilderment vanished and the beaming grin was back. "Oh I don't care." He grabbed Evelyn and spun her around in one of his great bear hugs. "I'm gonna be a father!"

I looked at Max across the table from me and winked. "I guess their day went well."

25

There was a bit of a chill in the air the next morning but I had learned that once the sun began its journey, the chill would fade and the day would warm nicely. Spring was a beautiful time in Ireland and held so much promise. I buttoned my sweater before I put my hand in Max's hand as we started a morning walk.

We neared the castle and stopped to admire the shamrocks that Finn and I had planted. They seemed to be doing well.

"Should we look for a lucky four leafed one?" Max asked.

"You won't find one," I said squeezing his hand. "Finn said while shamrocks may be related to clover, they only have three leaves." I plucked one and showed him.

"So where do the Irish get all their luck?"

"The same place any of us gets it. From the good Lord."

"Amen to that," said Max.

We walked a bit farther and turned toward the flower garden. I could sense something was on his mind. When we got to the bench in the garden, I motioned to Max that I wanted to sit down.

"Something's bothering you, Max. I can sense it." I searched his face but for once, I couldn't find any of the characters, Clooney, Columbo or Bogart, who usually showed themselves. This was just pure Max.

He pushed a couple of leaves aside with his foot. "I don't know how to tell you this."

My heart was doing flips. Tell me what? This didn't look like another proposal and one I might be closer to accepting. This looked sad.

Max took both my hands in his. "I have the prospect of starting my own PI firm. There have been several people who have inquired if I was interested in taking on some cases." He looked down at our hands clasped together and then back up at me. "I love being with you. I hate being apart but I'm not a handyman. I'm an old cop who can't get the urge to investigate and solve cases out of my system. It would mean I would have to travel, sort of an international investigator. And that means I couldn't be with you as much as I would like." He paused as if he wasn't sure what he wanted to say next.

"I understand," I said trying to keep a stiff upper lip. "I saw you come alive when we had a mystery here to solve. It's who you are. You can't stop being who you are."

He chuckled. "Like you can't stop being a sleuth?"

I shoved his shoulder gently with mine. "I do have to admit I enjoy the challenge."

"I know," he said as he took a deep breath. "That's why I would be so pleased if you would join me. We are a good team. We can pick and choose our travel time and I can do some of the cases on my own if necessary. I know with a grandbaby on the way, you don't want to be away from Evelyn too much." His face revealed his eagerness.

"I. . .I'd have to think about it." I looked down, not able to meet his gaze. I bit my lip harder to keep it from trembling.

"You have plenty of time." Max rose and pulled me to my feet. "I need to go back home to the States and figure out all the necessary licensing, etc., to make it legal. I have a friend, a lawyer, to help me with that so I need to leave for a while but I'll be back for your answer and certainly back for that little one to arrive."

I smiled. He had changed some from the Max I first knew. He was taking things a bit slower and he was thinking of me and my feelings. Yes, I was falling in love but now this was a whole new twist to our relationship for me to contemplate.

I reached in my pocket and pulled out the shamrock I had picked to show him the three leaves. "It's not a lucky clover, but maybe it's a lucky shamrock." I gave it to him.

He took me in his arms and kissed my forehead. "You are all the luck I need. I love you."

I looked up into those Clooney eyes. "I love you too."

Author's Note

Ireland was one of my favorite places in the world to visit. Like Casey, I was amazed at how green it was. Dingle, the town where the story takes place, is a real place on the southwest corner of Ireland. It is the only town on the Dingle Peninsula and is in Kerry County. It is near the area where a number of Irishmen are trying to keep the old Gaelic language alive. It took us by surprise one day while we sat on the porch of a café sipping tea as an older gentleman tipped his hat to us, rattled on in Gaelic, smiled and then went about his business. I think it was a friendly encounter. But I digress.

In the Dingle Bay, there truly is a dolphin who has been there for years. At last I checked, Fungie was still there performing jumps and playing in the wake of the tour boats that go out to greet him.

While we did not stay at a B&B with a castle attached to it, we did stay in a wonderful place that sat on a slight rise above the quaint town. The castle on the cover is the Leamaneh Castle that sits on the edge of the Burren in County Clare. It dates back to the late 1400s and is said to be haunted by a woman named the Red Lady who was someone to be feared. Servants who did not meet her standards were hung out the windows.

Pubs were the place to eat. Nothing fancy but good comfort food was always promised. Like Casey, I did not like the Guinness either. It has a strong flavor and gave me a stomach ache but it lends a great taste to the stews and other dishes that the Irish prepare with it.

Yes, there were crown jewels and they were stolen in 1907. There were no crowns among them and they were not even associated with any coronations. The collection included a jeweled star, five gold collars and a diamond brooch all belonging to the Order of St. Patrick. They were stored in a safe in the library at the Dublin Castle and the keys entrusted to Sir Arthur Vicars. Vicars claimed to have lost the keys. They were found by a maid but then shortly after, the jewels were discovered missing. Vicars claimed the thief was Francis Shackleton, a herald and brother to the famous explorer. Despite Shackleton's bad reputation, Vicars was still considered the main culprit. He was removed from his position and took up residence at an estate in Kerry County where he was eventually killed by the IRA in 1921.

Francis Shackleton was considered a more likely suspect. He disappeared after a stint in prison in 1915. The jewels have never been recovered and it is assumed that they were probably broken apart and sold. There are a few more times that Shackleton surfaces but under the name of Mellor and is buried in Chicester under that name.

I stumbled across the story of the theft of the jewels as I was looking for ideas on which to base my novel. Dingle was chosen as the town to set the story because it was one of my favorite places to visit. While there were many castles we visited, the picture of Leamaneh Castle just seemed to fit. All the rest is fiction with a little of the truth from the jewel theft woven in. Except for Fungie. He is for real.

If you'd like to learn more about our trip to Ireland, go to my website at www.karenrobbins.com and the page labeled Travel Posts Index. Click on Ireland and several pages of posts will be available to you.

It was a wonderful trip and fun to revisit through the eyes of Casey.

Books by Karen L. Robbins

Fiction

Hidden In Harper Valley
The Christmas Prodigal
Fort Lonesome
Letters From Santa
A Pocketful of Christmas
In A Pickle, Annie Pickels Series Book 1
Pickle Dilly, Annie Pickels Series Book 2
Ruby, A Novel
Divide The Child

Casey Stengel Mystery Books:
Murder Among The Orchids
Death Among The Deckchairs
Secrets Among The Shamrocks
Abandoned Among The Apple Trees
Perjury Among The Pickleballs

Non Fiction
A Scrapbook of Christmas Firsts
A Scrapbook of Motherhood Firsts

Made in the USA
Columbia, SC
12 May 2024

35189071R00104